OVER THE EDGE
FLYING WITH THE ARCTIC HEROES

OVER THE EDGE

FLYING WITH THE ARCTIC HEROES

K. C. TESSENDORF

ILLUSTRATED WITH
PHOTOGRAPHS AND PRINTS

ATHENEUM BOOKS FOR YOUNG READERS

Atheneum Books for Young Readers

An imprint of Simon & Schuster Children's Publishing Division

1230 Avenue of the Americas

New York, New York 10020

Book design by Patti Ratchford

The text of this book is set in Electra

Printed in the United States of America

First Edition

10 9 8 7 6 5 4 3 2 1

Library of Congress Cataloging-in-Publication Data:

Tessendorf, K. C.

Over the edge: flying with the arctic heroes / by K. C. Tessendorf

p.   cm.

Includes bibliographical references and index.

ISBN 0-689-31804-9

1. Polar regions—Aerial exploration—Juvenile literature.

I. Title.

G599.T47   1998

910'0211—dc21

97-34768   CIP   AC

To Marlis and Marcia,
the two ladies in my literary life

TABLE OF CONTENTS

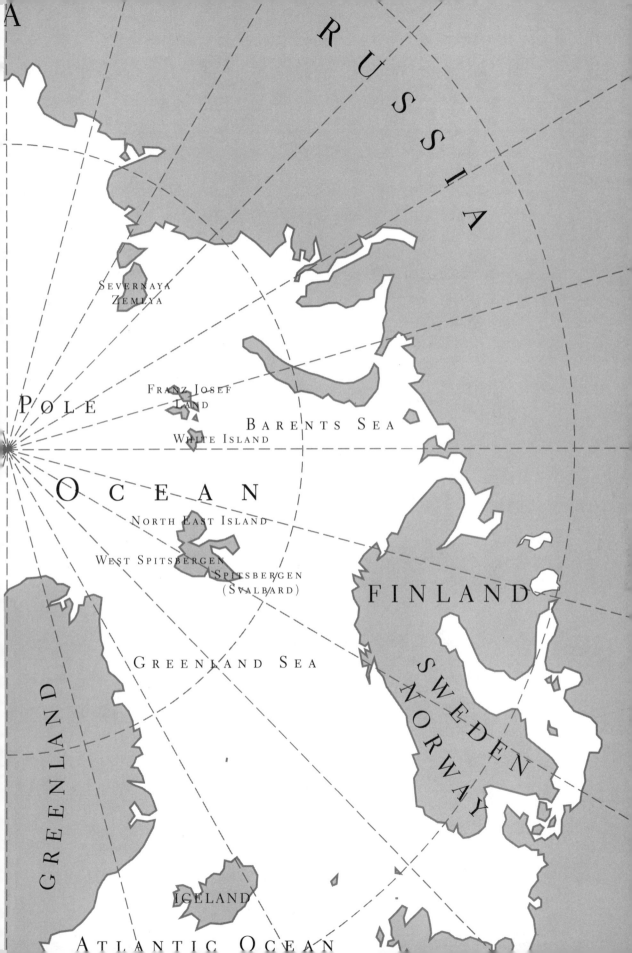

THE THING IS SO
DIFFICULT THAT IT IS
NOT WORTH
ATTEMPTING IT.
THE THING IS SO
DIFFICULT I CANNOT
HELP ATTEMPTING IT.
—*SALOMON A. ANDRÉE*

A SCENE AT THE EDGE OF A MILLION SQUARE MILES OF POLAR ICE. SHARP-EDGED ICE CAKES MERGE, IN THE BACKGROUND, INTO A FROZEN MASS ROUGHENED BY PRESSURE RIDGES AND VEINED BY SEMI-OPEN LEADS. *(Library of Congress Collection)*

THE EDGE

THE EDGE IS THE RIM OF THE MILLION SQUARE MILES of ice pack that permanently floats in the Arctic Ocean surrounding the North Pole. The South Pole is located in the land mass of Antarctica, but there is no land under the ice in the Arctic. This frozen mass is not static. Shifting position and surface day by day, jamming or tearing, this great ice barrier kept humans from reaching the North Pole for a long time. The Edge, then, became the symbol of trials and trouble to all those who dared to venture beyond it.

A very early voyage to the Edge occurred about twenty-three hundred years ago. The Greek astronomer Pytheas decided to sail as far north as possible. He traveled out of the Mediterranean Sea into the Atlantic Ocean and on past the British Isles to reach uninhabited Iceland, which he named Ultima Thule. Slightly beyond, Pytheas was halted by the Edge. He returned and reported his wondrous discoveries. Probably his learned countrymen passed off his account of a seaborne ice barrier and of glittering ice cliffs, ashore and afloat, as sailor tales. In any case, ice had no commercial value.

Five hundred years ago, Europe's growing taste for scents, spices, and soft fabrics only available in "the Indies" led to new thoughts of far-north travel. The Moslem empire blocked direct eastward passage to the luxury markets; but traders knew the earth was a globe and they tried to find a short route westward or eastward across the northern latitudes. Their search for a northwest or northeast passage to the East Indies was not from interest in polar exploration. They only hoped to squeeze by below the Edge. Despite efforts over more than two centuries, they did not succeed. Climate and conditions were too difficult.

In the nineteenth century, the heart of Africa, the Amazon rainforest, the high mountains and plateaus of Asia, and the outback of Australia were penetrated and explored by European adventurers. Only the two polar regions were left to scientists and explorers. Because the North Pole was nearer to the centers of civilization and offered fairly close-up land bases, it received the most attention. Who, representing which European nation, would be the first man at the North Pole?

The North Pole is located at the top of the world, 90° north latitude above the 0° equator (40° north bisects the U.S.), and a gauge of how far north human adventurers went can be shown by the degrees of latitude reached.

A few highlights of this quest: The Vikings settled southern Greenland in A.D. 986 and are believed to have sailed north on Greenland's west side to about 75° north. In 1597 a Hollander, Willem Barentz, while seeking a northeast passage above Asia, discovered the islands of Spitsbergen north of Norway and reached 80° north. That record stood until 1827 when Englishman William Parry crossed the Edge near Spitsbergen and slogged toward the Pole with dog teams and sleds, reaching 82°45' before the difficulty of rough ice travel exhausted the party and they turned back. In 1883 Adolphus Greely led a U.S. Army expedition in northwest Greenland and adjacent islands that reached 83°30'. Most of Greely's corps suffered and died before a rescuing party found them.

Fridtjof Nansen of Norway took the well-stocked, reinforced vessel *Fram* north near Spitsbergen and deliberately allowed it to be frozen into the expanding ice pack as winter arrived. He hoped that the ice floating on undersea currents would drift his expedition near the Pole. The ice-locked *Fram* did drift north, to 85°57' (1893–95). From there Nansen attempted to march to the North Pole, and reached 86°14' north before ice barriers exhausted the explorers.

The perimeters of polar expeditioning were clear: Approaching the Edge on the ocean was relatively swift, if mildly dangerous. Climbing over the Edge and proceeding across the ice pack was slow and torturously hazardous. The sea currents beneath the ice, and wind pressures above it, compacted the ice, raising it in jagged, jammed ridges that men had to crawl over. Then, these natural pressures wrenched the ice apart, leaving open water "leads" to be crossed or detoured. Ice near leads was treacherous, and weak ice could dump the unlucky trekker into the frigid sea.

By the 1890s there were a few visionaries who dreamed of making a passage on that other ocean, the air. Primitive gliders were the only winged aircraft, but balloons had been in use for a century and their ability to fly nonstop for long distances had been often shown. There was the unsolved problem, however, of how to steer them.

Then one fanatical optimist moved from "what if?" toward "let's get started!" He and his companions would find out if aerial arctic navigation in a balloon was possible. The aerial approach opened a new chapter in polar exploration.

CHAPTER ONE

THE *EAGLE* VANISHES

IN 1895, WHEN IT SEEMED EXPLORERS WERE CLOSING IN on the North Pole, an English journalist penned an article, "How to Reach the North Pole," gathering the views of past and aspiring explorers, including a Swedish gentleman with a radical approach. Salomon Andrée reported that his plan to float in a balloon on the ocean of air currents up to the Pole and beyond was well underway.

The next year he intended to lift off from the handy European arctic islands of Spitsbergen (now Svalbard) and ride a reliable south wind 715 miles to the Pole in perhaps ten hours (land expeditions might slog four to five miles a day). Such speed depended on Andrée's balloon being pushed by gale-force winds. Puffed along by average breezes, the aerial voyage would last about forty hours, still an amazing feat.

If his three-man balloon trip continued over to Alaska as he hoped, they would travel at least 2,200 miles. The balloon would be able to stay aloft for thirty days, claimed Andrée, and they would carry provisions to sustain them for much longer than that.[1]

Other Swedes have characterized Salomon Andrée as "a typical Smålander."[2] Individuals from the province of Småland stood out as hard-working achievers, proud and obstinate in purpose. It was said that by the time he was a teenager,

SALOMON A. ANDRÉE, THE STUBBORN
VISIONARY. (*Smithsonian Air and Space
Museum*)

student Andrée might have worn out a pair of soles marching up and back to accept school awards. The scholar became an engineer interested in applied science.

At twenty-two, Andrée journeyed to America, where science exhibits at the 1876 Centennial Exposition drew him to Philadelphia. Young Andrée was interested in the theory of using wind currents for commercial balloon transportation of passengers and freight, so he sought out the venerable American balloonist John Wise. The impressionable Andrée was not put off even though his one opportunity to ride with Wise vanished when the balloon exploded during gas inflation.

It may be that Andrée's attraction to polar ballooning came out of Wise's visionary ideas. The twenty-year veteran had proposed transatlantic ballooning and did make one attempt to fly to Europe, which failed before the balloon left North America. In 1879 Wise wrote in the *New York Times* about arctic air exploration. He thought that the solar heat of the twenty-four-hour summer sunshine would heat the air over the polar cap, causing it to rise. Cooler air would rush in under the warm mass, causing air currents upon which balloonists could ride into the polar region. That year also marked Wise's disappearance over Lake Michigan.

In 1882 Andrée signed on with a Swedish meteorological expedition, which stayed a year at Spitsbergen studying polar atmosphere. That expedition's director, Dr. Nils Ekholm, must have been mightily impressed by Andrée. Thirteen years later he agreed to accompany him in his North Pole attempt. After Spitsbergen, engineer Andrée obtained a position in the Swedish patent office. From that vantage point he talked a Swedish science foundation into funding an experimental balloon for him in 1893.

To prepare, Andrée went up briefly twice with a Norwegian balloonist. After that he boldly soloed on all nine flights that his balloon *Svea* (Sweden) completed. The most hazardous trip carried him across the Baltic Sea to a Finnish island.

Andrée experimented with sails and with heavy rope drags across the surface of the water to improve steering. The rope drags were set out to either side of the basket to be lowered for alternately braking the balloon and maneuvering it into turns. He claimed success in changing *Svea*'s direction up to twenty-seven degrees, when using the drags on the sea in ideal conditions, and predicted success on the ice pack.

Andrée's breakthrough into arctic ballooning came when Sweden's most prestigious explorer, Baron Nordenskiöld (first to sail all the way over Asia below the Edge) sought Andrée's advice. The baron was only considering using ship-tethered balloons to observe the ice pack or coastline; Andrée, however, brought up his North Pole dream.

"Well, that does not sound bad at all," responded the great one, who then passed the word in high places.[3] Superrich Alfred Nobel, who created the Nobel prizes, soon appeared at Andrée's office, and his hefty donation started the fund that built Andrée's balloon and paid for everything else. Sweden's King Oscar

THE FATED TRIO—FRAENKEL, ANDRÉE, STRINDBERG—POSE ENROUTE TO SPITSBERGEN (LUCKY ALTERNATE SWEDENBORG AT THE REAR). *(Library of Congress Prints and Photographs Division)*

II made clear his patronage by contributing, and thereafter the fund was oversubscribed. In today's dollars, Andrée's polar balloon project cost about $300,000.

Andrée became a Scandinavian hero. He had progressed from daredevil to herald of a new aerial age. He was embarrassed by the praise and parades, for he felt he hadn't done anything so far.

At Spitsbergen a sheltered site was chosen on Danes Island, and a balloon enclosure was constructed. Hydrogen to fill the balloon was manufactured by mixing iron filings with sulphuric acid. The traveling, building, and balloon inflation used up much of the short arctic summer. About August 1, however, the balloon was ready to travel. For two weeks the crew members waited for a south wind that did not come, and then they had to go back to Sweden because their ship's insurance was expiring.

What a bitter pill for proud Andrée! But his backers and countrymen were supportive. A setback, not a failure. Nobel generously asked if a new balloon was needed. Andrée declined but acknowledged that improvements were necessary on his present model. Summer's experiences made him aware of some facts regarding arctic air survival.

Dr. Ekholm, Andrée's mentor meteorologist, declined to try again next year. The gasbag was too leaky, he said, to sustain travel for a month, and he had rethought his theory about arctic air currents. Now he doubted that direct wind could be found. More likely polar air moved in vaguely circular patterns. Also, the balloonists had noted that icy fog had overhung Danes Island for long periods, probably typical of weather over the ice pack. Wetness, frost, lack of heat from the sun because of the mists—all were factors that made ballooning there difficult or impossible.

Andrée went to Paris and had balloon maker Henri LaChambre enlarge the silken gasbag to enclose 176,582 cubic feet of hydrogen gas. The *Ornen* (Eagle) stood about one hundred feet tall and was able to lift about five tons. The bulk of the supplies—including three sleds, marker buoys, a boat, and canned foods to support the aeronauts for at least four months—was stowed below the gasbag in the gathering of heavy cord netting enclosing it. Below was an observation platform studded with scientific instruments atop an enclosed round cabin stocked with immediate supplies, including gourmet foods and beverages, and a cozy bedroom for one flier at a time. Andrée and friends would travel first-class.

The 1897 *Eagle* aeronauts were: Salomon Andrée, forty-three, born leader, tall and strong; Nils Strindberg, twenty-four, physicist and accomplished photographer who had been with Andrée in '96; and as Dr. Ekholm's replacement, Knut Fraenkel, twenty-seven, a husky and cheerful engineer seeking adventure. All were bachelors. Andrée had claimed he was married to science. Strindberg, though, had a sweetheart he planned to marry as soon as he returned.

In '97 the expedition reached Danes Island earlier in the year, found the balloon house had survived, and was able to set up for flight by the first of July. They had repeatedly varnished the six hundred seams of bag silk to prevent leakage, then had searched for stubborn leaks by laying gas-sensitive strips on the seams.

On July 6 they got south wind, a hurricane of a wind that bounced the *Eagle* about in its open-roofed shed, doing its seams no good. The aeronauts declined to use it as an express ten-hour trip to the Pole! In the early hours of July 11 a brisk south wind arose and sustained itself. Fraenkel and Strindberg were exultant, Andrée on the reluctant side. Finally, Strindberg told the leader that the gas pressure of the *Eagle* would never be better than that day. After mulling for a time, Andrée announced they were going and ordered the north side of the balloon shed torn down.

From a conversation at Danes Island with a journalist just prior to departure, the idea that Andrée was nearly resigned to a one-way balloon trip is evident. "When may we begin to hope to hear from you?" the journalist asked, to which Andrée replied, "At least not before three months; and one year, perhaps two years, may elapse before you hear from us, and you may be surprised by news of our arrival somewhere. And if not—if you never hear from us—others will follow in our wake until the unknown regions of the north have been surveyed."[4]

In the afternoon of July 11, 1897, the last ropes tethering the restless *Eagle* were cut. Up bounded the balloon; then a lick of wind rolling down the hill behind the balloon house swept the craft down. The crew desperately heaved out ballast bags, and though the gondola smacked the sea surface lightly, the *Eagle* recovered nicely and made off north at about twenty-five miles per hour.

It was then the ground crew saw that two-thirds of Andrée's prized drag lines had been left behind, caught on the rocks fringing the beach outside the balloon house. The heavy drag cords had been fitted with couplings so that the balloon could not be stopped by a snag far below, and the rock tangle had caused them to release right away.

As the balloon flew northward it climbed to about eighteen hundred feet, though Andrée had planned not to rise beyond the range of the drag lines, about eight hundred feet. As the *Eagle* vanished from the sight of man into northern mists, it was a free-flying balloon.

People in the northern parts of Europe, Asia, and North America that encircled the polar basin were well aware of the Andrée expedition and alert for sightings of, or messages from, the brave balloonists. Radio was not yet in regular use, but Andrée carried thirty-six carrier pigeons. Because of the distances and polar magnetism, which would confuse the pigeons' homing instincts, not much success was expected from them. But it was hoped that some pigeons might blunder through to settled parts with their messages.

On July 15 a Norwegian seal-hunting ship about a hundred miles northeast of Spitsbergen received an exhausted pigeon that flopped into its high rigging. The skipper, not knowing Andrée had departed, shot the bird for the dinner pot, but it fell into the sea and was abandoned. A bit later this ship came into hailing distance of another vessel, which passed news of the *Eagle*'s flight. The skipper thought again on the strange pigeon, turned back, and had the luck to sight the carcass afloat on the sea, retrieve it, and find Andrée's message in a capsule:

> July 13, 12:30 midday, Lat. 82°2', Long. 15°5' E., good speed to
> E. 10° S. All well on board. This is the third pigeon post.
>
> Andrée.[5]

So the *Eagle* had flown at least forty-six hours.

Thereafter it was open season in the northern hemisphere on strange pigeons, but no other Andrée bird ever showed up. All the world looked for the reappearance of the balloon with its trio of daring aeronauts. For months newspapers published accounts of imagined sightings.

A balloon that was reported afloat on the ocean north of Norway turned out to be a dead whale. A Swedish housewife plainly saw a balloon with draglines. A balloon was discovered in a Siberian forest. Cries for help and rifle shots out on the ice pack were heard on the east Greenland coast. No credence for any of these was established.

From Hudson Bay, Canada, came a tale that natives had been fired upon by four men descending in a balloon. The Eskimos had killed two and eaten them, while the others escaped. Andrée had come down in Alaska, an arctic postman solemnly stated, and joined in the Klondike Gold Rush. Ole Bracke, an eccentric Swede living in Iowa, telegraphed his homeland that he was in psychic contact with Andrée.

In the summer of 1898 Andrée search expeditions probed arctic Siberia, the Greenland coast, and most importantly all the food and shelter caches left for the balloonists on islands north of Spitsbergen. No sign was found, and the verdict of arctic veterans became that the Andrée expedition had perished. In 1899 and 1900 three of the twelve marker buoys Andrée carried arrived on the beaches of Iceland, Norway, and Spitsbergen. Two contained messages older than the pigeon post (the earliest noted "We are in the highest spirits."). The third was the large polar buoy meant to be deposited on the North Pole. It carried no message. Thereafter, nothing . . . for thirty-three years.

The arctic summer of 1930 was unusually warm. This produced two effects upon White Island, a small glacier-topped mass not far out from the northeastern corner of Spitsbergen. Its few stony beaches became temporarily accessible as their snow cover was reduced. The Norwegian sealer *Bratvaag* spotted a herd of walrus at rest on a beach, passed a bit further, and landed a slaughtering party. Ashore they discovered a tin can, then a part of a sled protruding from a wasting snowdrift. It was marked ANDRÉE POLAR EXPEDITION 1896. Their last camp was thus discovered, August 6, 1930.

A party of geologists aboard the *Bratvaag* organized an excavation. A clothed partial skeleton was identified as Andrée's. His hard-frozen diary was in a pocket. Next a crude burial cairn revealed the remains of Strindberg. Fraenkel's partial skeleton was frozen into the surface near Andrée's. The corpses had been roughly handled, torn by bears, probably in the summer thaw following their deaths. The remains of the brave trio and every available expedition scrap were removed to Sweden, where the joint funeral of

THE DEPARTURE OF THE *EAGLE* FROM SPITSBERGEN. (*London Illustrated News, July 31, 1897*)

Andrée, Strindberg, and Fraenkel was observed with reverence and pomp.

Restorers were able to decipher about ninety percent of the explorers' written records. About twenty prints were made from film found with the bodies. These photos lent a haunting visual dimension to the written re-creation.

The Andrée party had heard the whistle of gas escaping from the start. The trio's morale, though, was high as they moved in sunshine over the Edge north-northeast for five hours. But the leaking gasbag sank slowly, and when a weather

MARKSMEN FRAENKEL AND STRINDBERG POSE BY A SLAIN POLAR BEAR. *(Smithsonian Air and Space Museum)*

front of fog appeared before them, the aeronauts were unable to fly over it despite jettisoning most of the rest of their ready sandbag ballast.

Entering the dank mist cooled the balloon and made it sink even more. Soon it was weighted down by ice, as well. An easterly breeze came up that pushed them toward Greenland. The *Eagle* sagged lower despite their lightening it by jettisoning some expedition supplies such as the polar buoy. After twelve hours Andrée reckoned distance flown at 250 miles.

The second day they continued to travel west below one hundred feet in woolly grayness. The balloon sank until the gondola began bumping on the ice pack. They continued to bounce along till a diminished breeze allowed the *Eagle* to settle on the ice. Here, as his companions slept below in the enclosed gondola, amid a fog-shrouded silence, Andrée wrote philosophically:

> How soon, I wonder, shall we have successors? Shall we be thought mad, or will our example be followed? I cannot deny but that all three of us are dominated by a feeling of pride. We think we can well face death having done what we have done.[6]

A freshening west wind pushed the balloon off again, and with sunlight warming the gas and more jettisoning of weight, the *Eagle* moved nicely east-northeast, as Andrée experimented with the sails and the one remaining spliced drag line, till it snagged and was lost. Here the found pigeon had been released with others. Then fog returned and the balloon again descended. As the slapping of the gondola on the ice pack increased, Strindberg suffered motion sickness. The voyagers conferred, and when another period of sunshine raised the balloon and it flew north, Andrée vented the gasbag and the *Eagle* settled permanently onto the ice.

At 8:11 A.M., July 14, they were out of the balloon's cabin 480 miles short of the North Pole, 376 miles northeast of their Danes Island lift-off sixty-five hours and thirty-three minutes earlier. Three sleds were packed with supplies, including their boat, and Andrée, Strindberg, and Fraenkel set off for the arctic island of Franz Josef Land. Each sled carried about three hundred pounds. The wretched surface of the ice-pack, with its slippery ridges and open water leads, slowed the castaways' southward march. Also the ice was drifting, often foiling their plans by carrying them in another direction. During three months of exhausting travel each option closed. The diaries reveal great self-confidence, no dissension. The Andrée party scrupulously continued compiling scientific data.

Andrée anticipated freshening their diet from "wandering butcher shops"

ON THE MARCH, A BOAT WAS CARRIED FOR OPEN WATER CROSSINGS. (*Smithsonian Air and Space Museum*)

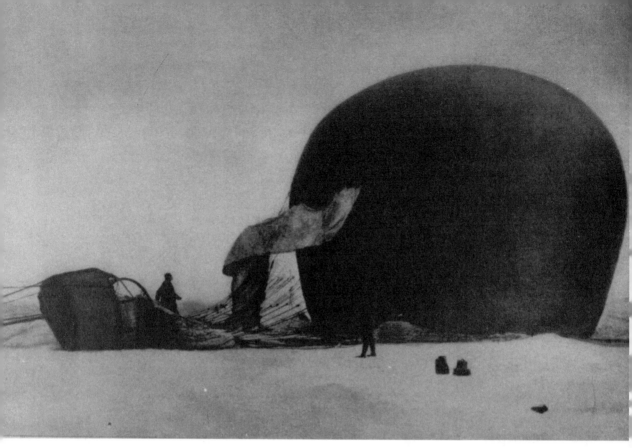

THE *EAGLE* DOWN ON THE ICE PACK 83°55' NORTH. *(Smithsonian Air and Space Museum)*

and was not disappointed. The ice-pack travelers did not have to hunt polar bears. The famished beasts sniffed warm blood on the breeze from miles distant and came to find their own meat supply. The trio shot thirteen bears and added seals and birds to the menu.

Andrée's party, according to his diary, consumed four to five pounds of meat per day per person. Quite a bit of the notes have to do with meal preparations—various ways to cook bear, the choicest cuts, best means of storage, and such. The travelers also ate raw bear meat. It is known from analyzed scrapings of a bear hide that they contracted trichinosis—an infection carried by bear flesh. Diarrhea and joint and foot pains characteristic of this disease are often mentioned, though not as disabling—except, possibly, at the end.

By hiking, or by the drift of the ice pack, the marooned balloon voyagers did travel south; but August's end, with the sun dipping below the south horizon, announced the approach of terrible cold and darkness. Since they could not reach an island shelter, they planned to winter on an ice floe. The trio set about diligently and confidently to build a large, comfortable igloo.

With no more tiresome travel, ice-pack life was eased. They had stockpiled enough meat to last them until April. And they still had a goodly amount of their original supplies. Their Primus stove was acting up, but all was generally well. An entry in Strindberg's supplementary log is devoted to the banquet prepared on September 18: "seal-steak and ivory gull fried in butter . . . wine . . . gâteau aux raisins . . . raspberry syrup sauce . . . port wine from King Oscar, vintage 1834 . . . biscuits and cheese . . . a glass of wine . . . festive feeling . . ."

Agreeably their ice floe moved south, and Andrée plotted it to pass down to the east of Spitsbergen. White Island came gradually into sight, looking inhospitable. They slowly passed east, giving it slight attention. The riders had adapted to igloo living. Then their ice floe pushed in close to the island and appeared to halt near a rare open beach. An island meant more meat opportunities, they rationalized, and Spitsbergen was just forty miles away.

But at 5:30 A.M., October 2, their floe shattered with a spine-chilling *c-r-r-r-ack* and split away a wall of their home. They had to scramble to rescue their scattered goods and then to undertake their final option. They went ashore and set up a balloon-fabric tent until they could build another igloolike shelter on the barren island. The final words of Andrée's main diary are: "No one had lost courage; with such comrades one should be able to manage under, I may say, any circumstances."

Thereafter diary entries become sparse and half illegible. A final dated entry, October 17: "Home 7:05 A.M." It is not known how the writer, Strindberg, died— by accident, or trichinosis? Andrée and Fraenkel, last of the valiant first fliers over the polar wastes, are believed to have expired soon after burying their comrade. It is probable that they—comfortable in the sealed tent—drifted into a deep death-sleep caused by carbon monoxide leaking from their faulty Primus stove.

CHAPTER TWO

WALTER WELLMAN'S BIG BUST

"WILL OUR EXAMPLE BE FOLLOWED?" WROTE ANDRÉE, isolated in the chill fog on the polar ice pack. Already, in 1894, an American, Walter Wellman, had begun negotiating with the French balloon maker Godard for a polar flight balloon. When Andrée announced his plans, Wellman waited to see how the Swedes would do. Their arctic disappearance changed the American's mind. But when dirigible motor balloons became available nine years later, Wellman's urge to fly to the Pole revived. Wellman resembled Andrée in two ways: He was brave and stubbornly tenacious, and he always had funding for his dreams.

Though a committed family man with five daughters, Wellman agreed to do stunt journalism for his newspaper, the *Chicago Record-Herald*. In 1891 he had gone to the Bahamas and, amid reams of news copy, pinpointed the site of Columbus's first landing on the island of San Salvador. The *Chicago Record-Herald*, pleased with increased readership, encouraged him in further adventures. Modern technology would soon allow conquest of the North Pole, and Wellman decided he could tackle the arctic and write about it. Indeed, why not Wellman first at the Pole?

Funded by his newspaper and other supporters, Wellman was off in the spring of 1894 aboard a Norwegian ship that ferried his party to the ice pack just north of Walden Island, Spitsbergen. He planned to walk to the North Pole. The expeditioners were off-loaded and the ship retired to shelter behind a big, grounded iceberg. Immediately a savage northwest gale began, and the nearby pack ice pushed forward and impaled and crushed their ship, which lingered on the surface only because it was wedged in the ice. Wellman returned to it and pulled off his trunk. It contained, amid much else, a set of evening clothes!

Wellman, never lacking courage against odds, continued to attempt to get onto the ice pack. It defeated him. Wind pressure piled a jagged jumble of ice, raising the Edge. Then slush created by a warm spell made travel impossible. At the

BRAVE, TENACIOUS WALTER WELLMAN WAS A FIVE-TIME POLAR LOSER. (*Library of Congress Prints and Photographs Division*)

last, hapless Wellman shot the dogs. Then he and his companions paddled in salvaged lifeboats south along the wild coast seeking rescue, which came, luckily, by way of a sealing vessel. Having sampled the hell of arctic ice, Wellman stopped at Paris to see about flying over it.

After the *Eagle* vanished, though, the *Record-Herald* approved a new Wellman land expedition for 1898: He would search for Andrée in the arctic island cluster of Franz Josef Land, winter there, and make a dogsled run for the North Pole in springtime when ice-pack travel conditions were believed to be best. Wellman started island hopping northward on February 18, 1899. Misfortune marched alongside.

Wellman, out for an unarmed camp stroll, met a polar bear that swatted him flat and prepared to devour him. Luckily camp dogs ran to the rescue; they surrounded the bear and held him there until the marauder was shot. In his memoir Wellman reminisces: "'In another moment,' I said to myself, 'he will have my head in his mouth.' But he didn't . . . I had only a lame shoulder and a scratch on the neck, while the bear's skin, made into a rug, lies under my feet as I write."[1]

On March 17 the explorers left the islands behind, moving on into the unknown across the ice pack. Three days later Wellman slipped a leg into a crevice while pushing at a stuck sled. He broke a shin bone. The leader's stubborn tenacity was asserted—they would go forward anyway. Rationally, he was insuring his death, but for a saving event two days later. Wellman recalls the "ice-quake":

> At midnight we were aroused by the ominous sound of ice crushing against ice . . . In an instant all five of us were outside the tent. We could see nothing. The storm had blown up again, and the air was filled with drifting snow. Two men were detailed to make a reconnaissance, the others creeping back into the tent out of the blast. But in two or three seconds there came another movement of the ice; another low, sullen rumbling sound.
>
> A crack opened directly under our sleeping bags, and in its black depths we could hear the waters rushing and seething. Running out of the tent into the darkness, one of us stepped into an opening, wetting his foot, and no sooner had he withdrawn his leg than the crack closed like a vice, and with such force that the edges of the blocks were ground to fragments and the debris was pushed into a quivering ridge. Ten feet away lay a dog . . . as neatly beheaded as if an executioner had done the job.[2]

Since the expedition lost about a third of its gear and supplies in the midnight ice smashup, they had to go back. And over those 140 miles Wellman's leg swelled disablingly. Fortunately they had posted a doctor at the base camp in Franz Josef Land, and he barely saved the leg from amputation. Wellman was about two years convalescing and thereafter walked with a cane and a limp.

By 1905 the steerable motor balloon dirigible had evolved, and the North Pole still remained unreached. Walter Wellman, having caught arctic fever, organized a polar expedition by dirigible. To the financial backing by newspaper multimillionaire Victor Lawson, President Theodore Roosevelt lent his enthusiastic vocal support and the motor balloon *America* was built in Paris.

It was basically a balloon modified into a dirigible fitted with a sizable rudder. Underslung by a long narrow cage, it was driven forward by one or more propellered gasoline engines. Rising and descending remained dependent upon removing ballast to gain altitude and gas-valving, releasing gas to lose altitude. However, aerial gasoline engines were frail and not fail-safe. And how long the gasbag could last was not known.

In 1907 *America* was the second largest motor balloon, after the one built by the German Count Zeppelin. It was 185 feet in length and had a maximum diameter of 52 feet and a volume of 258,500 cubic feet, with lift capacity of 19,000 pounds. The gasbag weighed a ton and a half; the 115-foot steel deck cage and its tube fuel tank weighed 8,500 pounds. When the tank was filled with 1,200 gallons of gasoline, another 5,000 pounds were added. The rudder, 900 square feet, weighed only 30 pounds.

A seventy-horsepower engine and two propellers moved *America* at modest speeds, below twenty-five miles per hour. The deck cage could carry a dozen dogs as well as the several crewmen. Wellman's dream airship carried enough food to sustain the travelers for months, plus survival gear if a march on the ice pack was necessary. Wellman believed, however, that *America* was able to stay aloft more than a week. In addition to six hundred pounds of supplies within reach of the deck cage, a trailing drag coil was designed to haul twelve hundred pounds of packed supplies.

This "equilibrator," as Wellman termed the spectacular device, was untried. It was an Andrée idea. The half ton plus of sheathed ballast was designed to trail smoothly upon any surface, its long, slender, snakelike bulk partly dragging and partly lifted in suspension (below 500 feet) attached to the airship. Proper handling of the equilibrator was expected to ease the problem of keeping *America* at a sustained altitude. Unwanted lift when the sun heated the gas could be controlled by raising more of the weight of the equilibrator above the surface. Similarly, if the airship sank, more of "the snake" could be trailed on the surface to take the weight of the gasbag.

In the spring of 1906 the airship expedition went to Andree's former site on Danes Island, renamed Camp Wellman. Because of weather, balloon-house construction delay, faulty engine and propellers, the *America* didn't fly at all that first year. They were back again in '07, but the Spitsbergen weather demons churned out the worst season in thirty years. Right off, the balloon house was blown down. It was rebuilt and the *America* readied, but gales blew right up to September 2. Although the winds then calmed, summer was over. It was too late to prudently launch a polar flight.

Characteristically, the leader decided to go anyway. A German vessel sent to spy on the operation towed the tethered *America* out to the center of the bay

THE GRAPHIC

AN ILLUSTRATED WEEKLY NEWSPAPER

The entire contents of this paper, both Illustrations and Letterpress, are copyright.

No. 1,975.—VOL. LXXVI.
Registered as a Newspaper

SATURDAY, OCTOBER 5, 1907

WITH COLOURED SUPPLEMENT
"*Pheasants.*"

PRICE SIXPENCE
By Post, 6½d.

THE GRAPHIC OF LONDON AWARDS WELLMAN FRONT-PAGE PUBLICITY. *(THE GRAPHIC, London, October 5, 1907)*

where the Americans cut loose and started their engine. Aboard were Walter Wellman, Melvin Vaniman as engineer, Felix Riesenberg as scholar (Columbia University), and ten sled dogs.

> With a thrill of joy we of the crew felt her moving through the air. Looking down from our lofty perch, we could see the equili-brator swimming along in the water, its head in the air, much like a great sea-serpent. . . . Soon the wind freshened from the northwest accompanied by snow. We were in danger of being driven upon the mountainous coast, which would mean the destruction of the ship and probably the loss of our lives as the steel car went tumbling down the cliffs into the sea.
>
> Everything depended on the engine. . . . Inch by inch we fought our way past the mountains, one after another, clearing the last by only a few rods. The open Arctic Ocean was before us; and well satisfied with the working of engine and ship up to this time, it was with great satisfaction I gave the order to Riesenberg at the wheel to "head her north!"[3]

But the snow squall increased its fury. *America* stood still, was pressed back. What a time, then, to find their compass had conked out! In the swirling blank whiteness, Wellman and friends were truly flying blind. Three times they dodged mountainsides abruptly emerging from the blizzard; then in a brief visibility break, the aeronauts saw a glacier surface between two mountains and went for an emergency landing there.

> But before we could descend upon the glacier we must drag our equilibrator, and also the retarder (which we had let down into the sea) up the face of the great ice-wall . . . rising nearly 100 feet sheer from the sea. . . . As the *America* swept over the glacier the two serpents crawled up the wall . . . at the top, they wound between and around giant rocks of the moraine . . . fell into deep crevasses in the ice, and then crept out again.
>
> . . . At the right moment the ripping knife was run into the sides of the huge envelope overhead, the gas rushed out, with a sigh the *America* gave up her life-breath, and settled on the ice.

JUST BEFORE DEPARTURE, SPITSBERGEN. NOTE THE "EQUILIBRATOR." *(Library of Congress Prints and Photographs Division)*

Rescue came from Camp Wellman support personnel and the ever-watchful Germans. The gasbag, instruments, and portable gear were salvaged and the steel cage left behind. So much for '07—but, of course, Walter Wellman would come back.

He stayed in the United States in 1908 to cover the presidential campaign. The following year, the veteran of the arctic fringe brought the rebuilt *America*, now with two motors and a floatable undercage, back to Camp Wellman, Spitsbergen. Despite the setbacks, Wellman attracted plenty of expedition financiers. Andrew Carnegie and J. P. Morgan were rumored to be minor investors. Nicholas Popov, a major backer, would ride along in 1909. In Russia his aristocrat family was so rich and tidy that they sent their soiled laundry to London for cleaning! Young Popov was an experienced balloonist and became an exhibition flier.

The Spitsbergen summer of 1909 was kinder and gentler. The *America* got away easily on August 15, pushed by a mild south wind. Aboard this ship were Wellman; Vaniman; Louis Loud, Vaniman's brother-in-law; Popov; and the dogs. This time the *America* zipped along at thirty miles per hour plus, flying rather high, as most of the equilibrator dangled. "So elated were we, one and all, that we hallooed to one another, and laughed, and cracked our jokes."

Spitsbergen fell behind. The happy fliers expected to be over the Pole in thirty hours. Ice cakes thickly flecking the dark green sea heralded their approach to the Edge. And just about there—

I saw something drop from the ship into the sea. Could one believe his eyes? Yes—it was the equilibrator. The leather serpent . . . parted within a yard of the top, and plump down into the ocean went 1,200 pounds of our balancing device and its contents of reserve provisions. Relieved of this load, the *America* shot into the clouds.

Our ears were ringing with the rapidity of our ascent. It was growing colder at this great altitude. Vaniman jumped for the valve line and pulled it far down to let enough hydrogen out of the top of the balloon to prevent us going to still greater heights.

Would the Arctics never bring me anything but bad luck? I sat there wondering if I had the right to take the lives of my crew in my hand by holding her head to the north, equilibrator or no

THE *AMERICA* NEEDED A TOW TO GET HOME IN 1909. *(Library of Congress)*

equilibrator. My own life, yes; theirs, no.

Vaniman sang out to me, "We'll have to fight our way back to Spitsbergen!" And in bitterness inexpressible, I told Popov at the wheel to turn her around and steer for Spitsbergen.[4]

But the south wind at five thousand feet blew very briskly, and the *America* was pushed backward north. Spitsbergen receded toward the horizon. They were over the ice pack and had to come down to manageable level, though the valving off of gas might cripple *America*'s means to get all the way back.

Amid Wellman's persisting "bad luck" there was always a guardian angel effect. Fortunately, a small Norwegian government marine survey vessel, *Farm*, was north of Spitsbergen. Observing the Americans' distress, *Farm* chugged up near the ice pack and awaited their slow coming. A line was secured, but the wind-bounced airship did not tow well and had to submit to the ignominy of being pulled back to Camp Wellman on the surface (this new cage floated).

The dogs, instruments, and records were ferried to the *Farm*, but the air crew proudly stayed with their ship. The Norwegian skipper wrote of his chill in seeing Walter Wellman settle into a chair and light up a big cigar a few feet beneath a gasbag yet holding perhaps one hundred thousand cubic feet of explodable hydrogen! The *America* was safely brought ashore at its home base.

Engineer Vaniman set about puncturing by pickax the fourteen gasoline tanks in the fuel tube. This progressive lightening unbalanced *America*; indeed, the frisky gasbag rolled about and escaped the cage. Up it soared, distending till—at an altitude guessed as six thousand feet—it exploded with the boom of many cannons. The floppy mass of fabric seemed to be descending directly above the *Farm*, and some crew members dived over the side in panic. The debris dropped into the bay nearby, and Wellman ordered it salvaged—for 1910, of course. . . . But upon returning to Norway, Wellman heard the worst: Robert Peary reported he had walked to the North Pole! (However, some present Arctic scholars believe he never reached the Pole.)

Instantly Wellman's zest for polar travel vanished. There would be little news value there for years. In 1910 a rebuilt *America* flew with Wellman from Atlantic City, New Jersey, bound for Europe! Well off the New England coast, the aeronauts were met by strong northeast winds that pushed them to a position midway between North Carolina and Bermuda, where the airship came down in distress. After a thrilling rescue of all personnel, Walter Wellman saw the derelict *America* blow away east into Atlantic emptiness, and with it his aerial obsession.

CHAPTER THREE

AMUNDSEN AWAITS ELLSWORTH

WAYWARD GASBAGS ASIDE, WHAT ABOUT AIRPLANES, THOSE descendants of the Wright brothers' 1903 heavier-than-air machines? Airplanes were still weak, wobbly, and short in range. In 1909 Louis Blériot of France successfully flew over the English Channel at its narrowest point: twenty-two miles.

Five years later technical improvements enabled a brave Norwegian, Lieutenant Gran, to fly nonstop from Scotland over the North Sea to Norway. He made it—three hundred and twenty miles in four hours and ten minutes—gliding gasless the last distance. Also in 1914, courageous Lieutenant Nagurski of Russia ventured out from Siberia in his frail aircraft over the frigid Barents Sea on air search missions. Nagurski's flights are believed to be the first ones north of the Arctic Circle.

The greatest of the active polar explorers, Roald Amundsen, secured for himself Norway's air pilot license Number One in 1912.[1] The famed conqueror of the Northwest Passage, and then the South Pole, was forty years old and not planning a pilot's career. He learned to fly to become the leader in polar aviation. Amundsen saw the vast opportunities of flying up there, surveying the unknown from above, moving in minutes over areas it might take weeks to cover on the ground.

Yet a dozen years would pass before Roald Amundsen got airborne in any significant way. The First World War brought arctic exploration to a halt. Later Amundsen's first aerial efforts from Alaska were fiascos, and his reputation was ruined because of business scandals. But then, counted out as a has-been, Amundsen regrouped and smashed by air into headlines again in the mid 1920s. He has been called "the last Viking" and his story *is* a saga.

In 1887, the year Roald Amundsen turned fifteen, his strong-minded, merchant-sea captain father died. His mother then busied herself in planning the future of her youngest son, the only one still at home. Loving

ROALD AMUNDSEN AT TWENTY-ONE WAS ALREADY AN EXPLORATION SURVIVOR. *(Library of Congress)*

her and wanting to please her, Roald did go through the motions of preparing for a career in medicine, but he had no intention of doctoring. Privately, he had decided to become a professional arctic explorer.

Decision is not commitment, and sometimes it leads no further than a dead end in daydreams. But Amundsen was rock solid in his commitment—he would make it happen against all odds.

He read and absorbed the literature on polar travel, and he applied himself to Norwegian sports, especially skiing, to toughen his body. At eighteen he planned and undertook his first expedition. Not far from Amundsen's Christiana (now Oslo) home, the Norwegian mountains were topped by a wilderness plateau called the Hardangervidda. Animals grazed there in summer, but the high plateau was empty in winter. Roald believed that no one had skied across it, so he talked a brother, Leon, into doing that with him.

What was planned as a two-day trip with an overnight at an isolated hut turned out to be a weeklong white nightmare. They were ill-equipped—without a tent—for the overnights in the open forced on them by a series of blizzards. Within a hundred yards of success, the brothers—lost in the snow swirl—turned back. Exhausted and unfed, they sought night shelter in the lee of a small peak. Leon simply crawled into his sleeping bag, while Roald burrowed completely into a snowdrift.

Body heat in the narrow snow cave at first caused a residue of melt; later the temperature dropped. . . . Roald then awakened because:

> My muscles felt cramped and I made the instinctive move to change my position. I could not move an inch. I was practically frozen inside a block of ice! I struggled desperately to free myself, but without the slightest effect. I shouted to my companion. Of course, he could not hear. . . . My shouts died quickly away, as I found it impossible to breathe deeply.[2]

Roald passed out. Luckily, he was dug out toward morning by Leon. A couple of days later they blundered back out at the farm they had started from, but were unrecognized because "our scraggly beards had grown, our eyes were gaunt and hollow, our cheeks were sunken, and the ruddy glow of colour had changed to a ghastly greenish yellow." Amundsen reported that in his future explorations, he was never in such immediate desperate conditions as during their cross-country ski fiasco on the Hardangervidda.

Roald's mother died when he was twenty-one, unaware that her doctor-son was about to be kicked out of medical school. Then Amundsen's move was onto the sea. In reading about polar explorations, he noticed that there often were squabbles between the expedition leader and the skipper of the ship carrying them. Amundsen planned to take on both roles himself. Also he became acquainted with the older Norwegian polar explorers, especially Fridtjof Nansen.

In a few years Amundsen succeeded in getting the first mate's job on a vessel carrying a Belgian expedition to the Antarctic region (1897–99). The ship became ice-trapped for a year. Illness laid low the skipper and expedition officers, and twenty-five-year-old Roald Amundsen became the able leader who got them out and back. His polar star was rising, though the Antarctic ordeal turned his hair gray at twenty-six.

With his rising reputation, Amundsen staked what wealth he had and could borrow by purchasing a small ship and three years of supplies, with the objective of finding a northwest passage between the icebound islands above North America. Amundsen found he was not a natural fund-raiser. He came up short of the needed money, and a principal creditor prepared to halt his departure.

Roald and his crew skipped. In the dark they sailed the little seventy-two-foot *Gjoa (Yew-ah)* away into the northern mists. "When dawn arose on our truculent creditor, we were safely out on the open main," Amundsen proudly recalled, "seven as lighthearted pirates as ever flew a black flag, disappearing on a quest that should take us three years."[3]

They wintered twice above North America. In the summer between, on August 26, 1905, the *Gjoa* slipped through yet another icy channel—then saw an American whaler ahead! They had found the Northwest Passage, achieving the goal (though of no commercial use) denied all others who had gone before over the centuries. The intensity of the responsibility upon Amundsen in navigating this final gauntlet of ice and rock reef left its mark on the steel-willed six-footer "in such a way that my age was guessed to be between fifty-nine and seventy-five years, although I was only thirty-three."

Amundsen's success was acclaimed worldwide, and he used his crest of popularity to write a book and lecture extensively, thereby paying off his long-standing debts. He then decided to try Nansen's idea of riding drifting polar ice to the North Pole, even acquiring Nansen's old ship, *Fram*. He was planning to sail down around Cape Horn and up the Pacific to start his drift north of Alaska. Then came the shocker: American Robert Peary claimed he'd walked to the North Pole (April 6, 1909).

That meant there would be skimpy book royalties and lecture profits from any North Pole expeditions for years. But Amundsen was ready and sailed anyway, though no one knew of his radical shift in plans. Roald Amundsen was bound for the South Pole.

The British thought that pole was theirs. An official expedition under Robert F. Scott, his second, was poised to start from Australia. From an Atlantic island Amundsen fired off his warning to Scott: "Beg leave to inform you proceeding Antarctica—Amundsen." The Norwegian reached the South Pole (December 14, 1911) thirty-five days ahead of the Englishman, who died of exposure on his return trek. Amundsen's practical operational know-how surpassed Scott's. Scott used ponies, tried primitive snowmobiles; Amundsen relied solely on dogs. He even factored them into the expedition diet:

> I planned to kill each dog as its usefulness should end for draw-
> ing the diminishing supplies on the sleds and its usefulness

should begin as food for the men. This schedule worked out almost to the day and the dog. Above everything else, it was the essential factor in our successful trip to the Pole and our safe return to the base camp.

When, as a hero, explorer Amundsen returned to reap his rewards by lecturing and writing about his South Pole triumph, Europe was moving into the distracting horrors of World War I. Norway remained neutral, and wartime prosperity came to the nation's shipping interest, in which Amundsen invested. When German submarines began sinking Norwegian ships trading with Britain and France, Amundsen denounced Germany and returned medals that that country had given him.

The Allies were alert to the propaganda value of showcasing VIPs on escorted tours of the western front, and Amundsen responded to that invitation. Passing through Paris, the Norwegian briefly encountered his own VIP of the future. Lincoln Ellsworth was a deskbound American airman who pleaded to Amundsen to include him in his next expedition. Unimpressed, the explorer politely evaded any promise.

As the war wound down in 1918, Amundsen departed on an attempt to sail around the world in the polar regions, starting northeastward from Norway above Asia and, after resupplying at Alaska, to reenter the ice pack with the hope it would drift the ship over the polar shortcut back to Norway. The expedition finally reached Alaska after two years' passage above Siberia, but Amundsen abandoned entering the ice pack.

Amundsen then thought to recoup his fortunes by a first-time flight from Alaska to Spitsbergen. He bought a long-range German airplane, but it crashed crossing the United States. Going further into debt, he bought a second aircraft and wrecked it in Alaska (1922–23). Thereafter his creditors closed in on the unlucky Amundsen, now bankrupt and verging on being a has-been.

"No one but a penniless explorer," he wrote ruefully, "can realize the frightful handicap from which nearly all explorers suffer in having to waste time and nervous energy in their efforts to raise the money to equip their expeditions."[4] Or pay them off afterward. Near the end of 1924, the hapless explorer, fifty-two, sat in a New York hotel room following an unsuccessful lecture tour. Amundsen reckoned that the incoming trickle of income would not clear him from his creditors till he was one hundred and ten years old! But his salvation was at hand. The telephone rang.

The caller said that he was Lincoln Ellsworth and that he had met the explorer in France. Amundsen, not recalling, was gruffly noncommittal. Then he heard the magic words: "I am an amateur interested in exploration, and I might be able to supply some money for another expedition."[5]

Ellsworth remembered the Amundsen he had met seven years before: "I saw a tall, long-limbed, rugged figure with a hawklike visage and eyes that bored through me and then seemed to look a million miles behind me into space."[6] Ellsworth was thirty-seven then, a nonflying paper shuffler in the American Air Service. Whenever he seemed to find a way out of his boring career, he hit a resistant wall—his father.

He was a rich man's child and heir. He had been a sickly youngster, "a fraidy cat," a bored dunce at a school he considered a jail. The boy was happiest alone in his room, lying on the floor staring at an atlas page, especially those spots marked "unex-

AMUNDSEN IN HIS PRIME, ABOUT THE TIME HE LEARNED TO FLY. *(Library of Congress)*

plored." His mother had died when he was small, and his father—an investor in mines, railroads, factories; a cosmopolitan traveler who owned a castle in Switzerland, a villa in Italy, and the only Rembrandt then in America—waited insistently for his boy to grow up and be like *him*. But Lincoln wouldn't, and the father-son battle of wills used up most of their life together.

As a young man, Lincoln was able to dodge much of what he thought dull in higher education, and with an allowance from his father went his own way. This led him to western Canada, where his aptitude in surveying work with railroads and city planners made him a good self-taught civil engineer. He also joined several expeditions that followed up where others had gone before. Occasionally he was called back by his father to work in family businesses. Then he'd break away again. . . . Many years slipped by.

In 1924, when Lincoln was forty-four, he approached his father,

LINCOLN ELLSWORTH, A MAN WHOSE DREAMS CAME TRUE. *(Library of Congress Prints and Photographs Division)*

seventy-five and ailing, about funding Amundsen so that Lincoln could go along as coleader of an expedition to fly to the North Pole. The senior Ellsworth's opposition seemed absolute. The father saw his participation as contributing to his son's death. At last, though, he buckled under and agreed to interview Amundsen.

"How vividly I remember that interview between my father and Roald Amundsen—the grim, old, white-faced financier facing the gray, bald but vigorous, weather-beaten old viking!"[7] They proceeded cautiously; Amundsen gave an excellent summation of the worth of polar exploration.

Then the old man jabbed. "Suppose I don't help you? What will you do?"

Certainly, Roald Amundsen was passing his hat, but he was a strong-hearted titan, too. With innate pride and grace he replied, "Well, Mr. Ellsworth, I will do what I have always done. I will get along some way."

It was the telling response, for James Ellsworth soon came around. He agreed to give $85,000 for aircraft and equipment. Within a day, though, he tried frantically to cut his son out of the arrangement, but did not succeed. Amundsen and Ellsworth's bold aerial adventure began.

CHAPTER FOUR

"THE DEAD RETURNED TO LIFE"

ROALD AMUNDSEN IMMEDIATELY SENT THE WINDFALL
$85,000 to Norway. Bankruptcy had not stopped him from securing, on an if-and-
when basis, the support of the Norwegian Aero Club for a flying polar expedition.
What Amundsen really wanted was a grand ride over the North Pole to Alaska in
a modern dirigible, but it was unlikely that even the Ellsworth bequest could pay
for that. So Amundsen decided to make do with two airplanes.

Amundsen cabled his trusted friend Lieutenant Hjalmar Riiser-Larsen of the
Aero Club and the Norwegian Navy. He asked him, as his pilot, to choose two
rugged airplanes for a reconnaissance flight to the North Pole. A versatile role was
expected for the second aircraft: It might become the rescuer of the other; or
become, when needed, a stockpile of supplies, parts, and fuel. The planes would
have to be big, powerful, long-range, and truly able to land and take off from ice,
snow, or water.

With these requirements in mind, Riiser-Larsen bought two Dornier Wals
(whales) at $41,000 each. Dornier was a German company specializing in flying
boats. After the Versailles Treaty forebade Germany to manufacture aircraft,
Dornier went abroad. The two Wals, N24 and N25, were assembled in Italy.

N25 GETS A HELPING SHOVE. *(Library of Congress)*

Riiser-Larsen and Lieutenant Leif Dietrichson, also of the Norwegian Navy, took delivery at a lake near Pisa after just one test flight. *N24* and *N25* were then dismantled and shipped to Spitsbergen. They would not be airborne again until they took off for the Pole.

The rugged Dorniers featured sturdy whalelike belly hulls of duralumin, an aluminum alloy. There were no landing fields where the Wals were bound, but they were built to be able to take off from reasonable surfaces of ice, snow, or water. This metal flying boat was fifty-two feet long, with a sixty-eight-foot wingspan. It weighed four tons and was designed to lift twenty-five hundred more pounds. In an era of uncertain motors, the Wals mounted the best: Rolls-Royce engines of 360 horsepower each, set back-to-back above the center wing. They could lift the aircraft to ten thousand feet and move it at ninety miles per hour over a range of up to fifteen hundred miles. All state of the art in 1924.

Meanwhile Amundsen felt easier about obtaining further financing, up to about $150,000, after his polar flight became an official Norway expedition. Parliament authorized a money-raising special stamp issue: Buyers sent in postcards to be ferried "to and from the North Pole" and, with the expedition imprint, the keepsakes would be mailed back from the Arctic. Income from the sale of publicity, books, photographs, and lectures would follow. So, in the manner of Andrée and Wellman, the Amundsen-Ellsworth expedition optimistically gathered at Spitsbergen in May of 1925.

The Wals were carefully fitted out on the snowy beach at King's Bay. Their engines were fussed over, and one taxi maneuver was made out onto the bay ice. Then the hulls were overloaded by nearly double the Dornier allowance with supplies for thirty days, as well as equipment for an emergency march to Greenland, but no dogs. For N24, it was Ellsworth up front, in the first open cockpit, as navigator; Dietrichson, pilot; Oskar Omdal, mechanic. N25's airmen: Amundsen, navigator; Riiser-Larsen, pilot; Carl Feucht, Dornier mechanic. On May 21 the weathermen predicted decent conditions and the Wals roared into a forty-five-minute warm-up.

N25 slid down onto the bay ice at 5 P.M. The overloaded plane bowed the ice and had to take off immediately. The Rolls-Royce engines strained near their maximum of 2,000 rpm as the heavy Wal moved over the level ice. Riiser-Larsen stared stoically as the glacier wall at the end of the fjord loomed before the speeding N25, and he hauled the Wal into the air at the proper moment. A relieved *ahhhh* arose from the watchers on the beach.

Meanwhile N24 seemed stuck on the beach, and the crowd surged to the tail and shoved. From the Wal's belly surface came the grating of tearing rivets. But N25 was rising in the sky and N24's Dietrichson vowed, "Now or never!" proceeding down onto the cracked bay ice, where standing water readily seeped into the plane's bottom. The pilot hoped there wouldn't be a sea landing, as he gunned the engines and skidded into a takeoff to join N25. The romantic Ellsworth felt "like a god" as they zoomed above the glacier and turned north.[1]

North of Spitsbergen, dense fog hid the approach to the ice pack and the Dorniers rose to three thousand feet. N24's pilot kept a worried eye on the engine temperature, which rose past 100 degrees even as mechanic Omdal worked on the motors. Up the mercury thread crept to 115 degrees—and burst the gauge. Dietrichson expected engine failure and descent into chaos, for his brief sighting of the sea revealed thick clusters of small ice cakes afloat there that would slash and tear the hull. . . . But the Rolls-Royces kept churning out their 360 horsepower thrust, and the pilot gradually relaxed. Dietrichson didn't know how the engines kept going—but one had to be a cockeyed optimist to be flying here in any situation.

Abruptly at 82° north the fog ceased and revealed a glaring white ice desert stretching to all horizons. N25 signaled (they had no radio link), and the two planes climbed near their top altitude, ten thousand feet (and N24's miraculous Rolls-Royces delivered this, too), to see more of the unknown. Amundsen, staring at that uncompromising surface, waxed philosophical, recalling the many it had claimed:

> What have you not seen in the way of need and misery? . . . What have you done with the many proud ships which were steered towards your heart never to be seen again? . . . No clue, no sign—only the vast white waste.[2]

Glaring hours passed in the twenty-four-hour sunshine as the two heavy birds droned on into a brisk northeast wind that forced a navigational drift they couldn't figure. The N25 pilot, Riiser-Larsen, napped momentarily in the monotony. Where were they going; what was their flight plan?

Amundsen's intention was that the Dorniers fly north till half their fuel was expended. Under ideal wind and navigation developments they would then be very near the Pole. The expedition would land on the ice pack and reconnoiter. The great explorer wished to pitch his tent right on the mark, as he'd accomplished it at the South Pole. After this triumph they would fly back in the two Dorniers, or, more likely, fuel would be cannibalized from one aircraft to ensure a plentiful supply in the Wal that would carry all back to Spitsbergen, or perhaps on to Alaska.

The expedition had been flying for hours over thoroughly inhospitable ice terrain—a rough-topped succession of close-set pressure ridges and adjacent ragged-edged gulches. Not a glimmer of water appeared in this ice desert. Then, at about 1:00 A.M., in the endless arctic summer day, mechanic Feucht reported half the fuel gone. Signaling toward his partner, Riiser-Larsen started N25 down to see up close what he could find for a landing area. N24's Dietrichson followed and was heartened to glimpse for the first time a blue spangling of narrow sea leads and meltwater ponds ahead. But instead of investigating these, N25 dropped down and entered a very questionable gulch. Dietrichson considered that Riiser-Larsen had gone mad!

He didn't know that one of N25's engines had abruptly quit. With the overloaded aircraft sagging at low altitude, Riiser-Larsen had to accept what was immediately before him—the gulch!—splashing down into a mixture of snow and slush. Fortunately the plane's clean, high wing cleared the ice ridges on

N24 AND *N25* MAROONED ON THE ICE. *(Library of Congress)*

either side as the Dornier careened dangerously down the length of the trough to bump up aslant on the blocking ice floe. No one was injured and the plane seemed okay, but at a glance, the prospect of flying out appeared to be nil.

N24 had to land now, too. After about ten minutes' searching, Dietrichson slid the Wal into a pond of meltwater on an unusually flat expanse of ice perhaps two miles from *N25*. As the plane skidded to a stop on the pond's far side, one of *N24*'s heat-worn engines ceased—and Omdal yelled that water was invading the belly. But if these problems could be solved, they might be able to take off from their site.

The crew tumbled out, floundering in two feet of snow. A curious seal slithered tamely out of the pond to inspect the aliens, and fuzzy-minded Ellsworth allowed a hundred pounds of fresh meat to creep away untaken. While Omdal worked on the engine and pumped water from the cabin, the others climbed ice hummocks and eventually spied the distant upward tilt of *N25*'s nose. With joy they saw figures moving there and hoped that those figures would soon see the Norwegian flag they had left erected on one the hummocks.

Over at *N25* they had determined their position as 87°43' north, a disappointing 150 miles short of the Pole, a result of the persistent northeast headwind.

Gauging the expedition's predicament, Amundsen turned his thoughts toward Greenland. But then his sighting of N24 plus Feucht's prompt success in repairing N25's engine widened their options. Since the word semaphored from the crew of N24 was of continuing engine failure and hull leakage, Amundsen asked them to come over. N25 had regained its mobility, and with six men as icebreakers, maybe an aerial escape could be worked out. They sorely needed help, too, to protect the plane from the ice shifts that seemed to be stalking it.

Ellsworth and Dietrichson had started to go to N25 right after they spotted it, floundered for a dismal half mile, and returned. After the contact, the crew of N24, weighted with supplies, slogged over a wearisome up, down, and far-around route through the ice labyrinth only to be stymied near their goal by an open water lead. They then had to travel back the same punishing route, altogether an exhausting eight-hour ordeal. When Amundsen messaged that the blocking lead seemed closed up, the men again shouldered their eighty-pound packs and skied out hopefully.

The lead near N25 had closed but its surface looked treacherous, so the men loosened their ski bindings for safety. Very cautiously they slipped on ahead in a line; Omdal, Ellsworth, and Dietrichson had this and only one other ridge to cross. Abruptly, the last man, Dietrichson, plunged up to his armpits in seawater. Ellsworth had scarcely turned his head when, with a cry, Omdal ahead also plummeted from view. The American felt his footing give—but slid nimbly sideways onto a provident block of solid, old ice.

The men wore buoyant jackets, an afterthought-purchase in Norway. However, powerful sea currents began to drag each of them beneath the ice.

Dietrichson was stretched with his toes bumping the ice's underside. Ellsworth now moved with cool dispatch, lying flat and extending his ski tips toward Dietrichson, who grasped them and was drawn closer. Breaking through the soft ice and struggling mightily, Dietrichson was finally hauled out, pack and all, onto Ellsworth's home plate of strong ice where he sprawled exhausted.

On the other side Oskar Omdal was in a bad way, with only head and hands visible, the latter lacerated by furious, desperate scrabbling to stay above the ice lip. The poor fellow had broken off front teeth on the ice, too. Now, as Ellsworth, flat on skis, wriggled like a seal toward him, Omdal hoarsely cried out in English, "I'm gone! I'm gone!"[3] In the nick of time Ellsworth grasped Omdal's pack straps and held him firm—all he could do until the revived Dietrichson crawled out and cut away the eighty-pound pack, setting it aside. Then the pair pulled out the bleeding, nearly unconscious Omdal.

ELLSWORTH SAVES THE EXPEDITION. HAVING RESCUED DIETRICHSON, HE MOVES TO GRASP THE DESPAIRING OMDAL. *(Library of Congress)*

The men of N25 heard the cries of their hidden comrades and, strapping on skis, started into the snow toward the obscuring line of hummocks. They met the survivors floundering over the crest, two without skis and stripped of their heavy packs. At Amundsen's camp, a change of clothes, bandaging, hot drinks, and especially the comradeship of the reunited group raised spirits; and the following long sleep mended bodies. Ellsworth had saved more than two lives—for all six were needed to hack, shovel, and build their way out of the ice.

N24 was abandoned because Omdal judged that the heat-worn engine could not be run dependably without an overhaul in a nonexistent shop. Too bad, because the terrain was better over there. Here N25 was in good flying condition but without a runway. Yet the ice field, responding to the thrusts of ocean and air currents, was reshaping itself all the time. Perhaps someday soon the ice would break apart and give them a nearby quarter-mile open lead of Arctic Ocean!

The expedition had reunited on May 27, six days out of Spitsbergen. How long could they wait?

The uninhabited north coast of Greenland was over four hundred miles away. There was hardly any hope of the six surviving such a march if ice-pack surface continued to be as rough as it was nearby. But there were men here who would prefer that effort to helplessly starving to death beside the plane. It would be foolish, however, to abandon N25 prematurely. Amundsen (who Ellsworth thought had aged ten years since Spitsbergen) ordered that rations be cut so that they might remain till June 15 and still, if necessary, make a march thereafter.

Then began the time of constant, often fruitless labor. Under the twenty-four-hour sun they could work as long as necessary. When the pick-and-shovel gang, exhausted, left off, they crawled into cramped quarters aboard N25, rather than into tents, because they liked the artificial darkness. High arctic summer on the ice pack brought temperatures just above—or as the sun swung down near the horizon, a bit below—freezing. The thawing snow surface caused ground fogs of clammy rawness, hampering visibility.

Always a night guard watched the treacherous ice, ever in slow motion, that seemed bent on nipping or crushing the flat-bellied Wal. Overnight, ridges raised or moved, and leads opened and closed. A new compression of the ice nearby brought N24 nearer and made it possible to salvage supplies and fuel from that now thoroughly ice-mired derelict.

The expedition had not been prepared for ice chiseling—yet, they must move hundreds of tons. They had three wooden shovels; a small hatchet; an ice anchor, swung as a club; plus sheath knives strapped to ski poles for chippers. The first ice ramp was built this way, and with ten hands pushing hard while Feucht's gunned the engines, N25 climbed out of its hazardous position onto a safe patch of ice. From there a possible take-off runway along a frozen lead lane could be reached if another six hundred feet of ice taxiway were cut, filled, and packed smooth. The ice gang began laboring on this, but as they slept, the lead closed up again.

In time wind and currents prepared another frozen lead nearby. An approach ramp was chipped out and packed smooth. Then all piled aboard as Riiser-Larsen proposed a takeoff try. But as the Wal moved down onto the lead, the ice gave way, and despite a roaring attempt at takeoff, all the Dornier did was ice-break down the length of the lead. They resolved to try again the next day. But as they slept, guard Feucht raised an urgent alarm. The shifting ice was squeezing the Wal's belly! Out spilled the crew, led by the burly Riiser-Larsen, wildly stamping and whacking the ice to blunt sharp edges.

"Another chapter for our book!" he wisecracked in a rare unsolicited comment.[4] The next takeoff attempt also failed because of breaking ice and lack of wind lift. They abandoned the dangerous lead.

"On May 31, when we had been prisoners for ten days, our chances for launching the plane were no better than the day we landed," commented Ellsworth.[5] Amundsen sought comfort in the axiom: "Patience—the explorer's indispensable salve."[6] Morale held despite the frustrations and failed attempts. There was little snapping and snarling among the overworked, underfed individuals. Four were Norwegians, silent people not given to making small talk. Feucht, a German who hadn't planned to fly with the expedition, was the most despondent, according to Ellsworth. Feucht also suffered the agony of an abscessed tooth, finally removed with a pipe wrench.

More failures followed as the June days passed. On June 2, James Ellsworth died at his villa near Florence, Italy, still trusting that in Amundsen's hands his son would emerge safely. In another takeoff attempt from a frozen lead, the ice held, but down the line of departure the lane curved slightly. The pilot had hoped to be airborne at that point but wasn't, so he cut the throttle to avoid having the plane skid to its destruction going around the curve. The Dornier settled heavily and while still at speed broke through the ice and nearly nosed over. Then there followed a strenuous work session to free N25 before the ice could solidify and imprison the plane.

Low-lying mists had prevented the crew from being able to see ahead. Fog or not, Dietrichson and Riiser-Larsen skied out each day to reconnoiter the ever-changing icescape. On June 6 when they were in the vicinity of N24 the vapors cleared briefly and the sun highlighted a plain of solid-looking ice at least eighteen hundred feet long. The pilots saw the possibility of a runway there, after the removal of two feet of soggy snow and the chipping away of protruding ice.

Getting there—about eight hundred yards—demanded building a ramp up onto an intervening floe, filling an ice ditch, cutting through a solid hummock of ice, and then dealing with another crevasse. All this roadwork just to approach the area where, by then, the shifting of the ice might have made it another road to nowhere. But Amundsen's men also realized that this was their last chance before the June 15 deadline, so they set to work with desperate enthusiasm.

At the start they had to work double-quick and overtime because a large iceberg, which they called "the sphinx," began to creep up on N25. After midnight, with the Wal moved safely above on the floe, all hands collapsed wearily aboard.

DIETRICHSON AND RIISER-LARSEN DUMP CARGO IN THEIR LAST CHANCE TO FLY OUT. NOTE RIISER-LARSEN'S GIANT FOOTGEAR. *(Library of Congress)*

When they woke up, the sphinx was crouching on the exact site the plane had vacated. The climax of the ice-escape program came in cutting a sixty-foot-wide path to clear the wings—as described by Ellsworth:

> It was a wall of ice fifteen feet thick. It took us an entire day to accomplish this—bitter work, on our knees, chopping with the pocket ax and the ice anchors, our legs wet to the skin from the melting ice, our hands, always soaking in the icy brine, red, raw, and swollen from handling the tools.[7]

Beginning June 10, they started shoveling the heavy wet snow from the runway. It was slow work, and at quitting time the exhausted men despaired because they had only cleared a hundred feet. Then Omdal came up with the saving inspiration: instead of three shoveling in shifts, let all six tramp it flat by squares to freeze as a hard, slick surface. And so it was done—*tramp, tramp, tramp,* for three days. On the evening of June 14, having reduced their load of expedition necessities by nearly a ton, all climbed aboard. Riiser-Larsen tried to take off on their tramped runway but it was sticky from daylong melting.

The quiet flier then offered a rare prediction: "We will do better next time."[8] Up very early, taking advantage of the overnight freezing, Riiser-Larsen gunned the Wal. It slid easily down the deteriorating but slick runway, gained enough speed to jump a widening seven-foot crevasse with ease, and—glory be!—*N25* was airborne after twenty-six days! "No take-off in the history of flying can ever have caused more satisfaction than this," affirmed arctic flier and historian John Grierson.[9] And surely the Amundsen-Ellsworth expedition had *earned* that passage.

Navigator Dietrichson set a return course that covered a new stretch of the white unknown, but the weather was dirty nearly all the way, with a brisk south headwind. As the fuel gauge dropped near zero, their eyes ached from searching ahead. Finally, *peaks* definitely spiked the horizon—Spitsbergen!

After the cheers, Amundsen announced the end of rationing and distributed a hoard of chocolate cakes. Ellsworth gobbled down seven of the sweets and immediately felt strange. Then the stolid Riiser-Larsen revealed that for the past hour he had felt the stabilizing tail controls tightening. *N25*'s return would have to end in a forced landing before steering the aircraft became impossible. The sea was rough, but the pilot's landing was perfect despite repeated duckings by icy seawater of those in the open cockpit. Ellsworth felt no anxiety— only chocolate-induced airsickness, then seasickness.

So the Amundsen-Ellsworth expedition of 1925 ended with the tough *N25* taxiing into a wild Spitsbergen cove one hundred miles from King's Bay. The castaways of the sterile ice fields went ashore to savor gravel underfoot, green plant life, birds winging and chirping. And their luck of June 15 yet held; within an hour a sealer sailed around a point chasing a wounded walrus and accepted with joy the six hitchhikers, who slept and ate voraciously as the little ship carried them to King's Bay.

It had been a month since the two Dornier Wals had first droned away into arctic silence. The Norwegian government had for weeks maintained a sea and air search below the Edge and were politely going on though hopes had faded. The U.S. Navy considered sending up its dirigible *Shenandoah* to scan the Greenland seacoast for survivors, but had not yet moved. To the world, the polar fliers had been consigned to join Andrée's balloonists in the arctic mysteries file. So they now became "the dead returned to life."

On July 5 the crew flew *N25* up the fjord to land in Oslo's harbor for their grand official welcome. They taxied in past the gathered naval might of Europe,

THE "DEAD RETURNED TO LIFE." LEFT TO RIGHT: RIISER-LARSEN, OMDAL, DIETRICHSON, AMUNDSEN, ELLSWORTH, FEUCHT. *(Library of Congress)*

saw cheering crowds at the wharves, and went on to accept the royal greeting. Ellsworth, who received a medal for bravery from the King of Norway, wept that his father had not lived to see this day.

The wealthy heir was thoroughly hooked on arctic exploration, and before the year was out he would buy a new dirigible from Mussolini and return with Amundsen to Spitsbergen in the spring of 1926. They planned a doubleheader then: first over the North Pole and then directly on to Alaska, a first crossing of the last vast expanse of northern white unknown.

It was good that on their festive day they had no inkling that two tenacious Americans, the U.S. Navy's Richard Byrd and Floyd Bennett, would be at Spitsbergen, too, and claim to snatch away the North Pole prize.

CHAPTER FIVE

BYRD AND BENNETT FLY TOWARD THE NORTH POLE

In 1926 THREE EXPEDITIONS WERE BENT ON THE AERIAL conquest of the North Pole.

At Spitsbergen, Amundsen and Ellsworth awaited the arrival from Italy of their new dirigible, *Norge*, aboard which they planned to capture the North Pole prize on the way to the greater triumph of a nonstop crossing of the Arctic to Alaska. Meanwhile in Alaska it was the intention of an Australian arctic explorer, Hubert Wilkins, to fly in an airplane eastward to Spitsbergen with American pilot Ben Eielson. And sailing north from New York came Commander Byrd's expedition. Richard Byrd and associate pilot Floyd Bennett were on leave from the U.S. Navy to make a privately backed attempt to fly a Fokker trimotor airplane round-trip to the North Pole from Spitsbergen—and they had to do it *first*.

Lieutenant Commander Richard Evelyn Byrd was not then a household name, though the navy was already aware of his presence and ambitions. And in background he was a Byrd of Virginia, where the family had been prominent since colonial days. Dick Byrd was the middle son in a Harry, Dick, and Tom trio. Harry was older, active in state politics, a future Virginia governor and U.S. Senator. He was above sibling rivalries. Dick and Tom were just a year apart, though younger Tom was bigger, which evened out their competition.

Both Byrd parents had strong personalities. The district attorney father fostered the natural rivalry between Dick and Tom as excellent training. To steel the boys' courage, their marksman dad had them hold up business cards as targets for him. Boxing was a basic home sport, with light Dick pushing to punch out six-foot-two, two-hundred-pound Tom. In summertime the brothers competed for their spending money, which their father tossed into a deep river pool. Tom was the stronger swimmer and thereby the richer, till Dick developed the capacity to stay underwater longer and intercept the coins as soon as they slipped below the surface.

The most important event of Dick's youth came in 1900 when, at the age of twelve, he convinced his parents, especially his mother, to allow him to travel alone to the newly acquired Philippine Islands to visit a family friend. The friend was a former associate of the elder Byrds and was now an army judge with the American occupation force. So young Dick crossed the United States by rail and boarded a transpacific army transport that, after outlasting a terrible typhoon, put him ashore in the Philippines.

Because many islanders had not greeted the occupation by the U.S. Army with enthusiasm, guerrilla warfare was widespread, and on its fringes Dick had thrills aplenty. Young Byrd's letters were published in a local newspaper, making him the war correspondent of Virginia's Shenandoah Valley. To keep him out of a cholera epidemic, Dick's host put him aboard an English tramp steamer that continued westward slowly, with many picturesque ports of call, eventually depositing the around-the-world traveler in Boston. He had certainly met the strict Byrd code of self-reliance.

As the trio grew up, Harry was all for public affairs, while Tom developed a keen businessman's sense. But Dick was "erratic," according to his father.[1] He wanted to be an explorer and impulsively wrote in his diary, at fourteen, that he would make himself the first man to reach the North Pole. A naval career would help, Dick decided, and the family obliged by seeing to it that he received an appointment to the U.S. Naval Academy (1908). The following year the navy's Robert Peary claimed the North Pole for America, and seemed to cancel out Byrd's fanciful goal.

At the academy, Byrd was a leading figure in sports and class activities, but trouble dogged him. As a 153-pound sophomore quarterback, he scored the winning touchdown against Princeton, but his foot was broken in three places as he crossed the goal line. Afterward, it was reinjured in a gymnastics fall. On a midshipman cruise Dick came down with typhoid fever and was hospitalized in England.

Then, on his first sea duty after graduation, Ensign Byrd fell down a battleship hatch, permanently damaging his game leg. The navy placed him ashore for headquarters duty, mostly public-relations work with Washington VIPs. This seemed a long way from the North Pole. When World War I opened new navy opportunities, however, Byrd, despite his limp, wangled pilot training. He became a good flier, and his leadership potential was tested as commanding officer of the small naval air force sent to Canada for antisubmarine duty.

His explorer spirit reviving, Byrd became involved in planning the 1919 navy project to fly the first airplane across the Atlantic Ocean. However, when the large NC4 flying boat succeeded in making a record ocean crossing, it was without Byrd aboard, though he had struggled to be there. After the war, Byrd was again assigned to headquarters public-relations duties, this time as lobbyist in Congress for navy causes.

Then the navy secured President Coolidge's permission for a 1924 launch of an Alaska–North Pole–Spitsbergen flight using its big dirigible *Shenandoah*, which would break all polar air records. Washington insider Byrd saw to it he was signed on. But this dirigible later suffered structural damage in a storm at its New Jersey mooring, and the arctic trip was wisely canceled. *Shenandoah* later broke apart in an Ohio thunderstorm.

Richard Byrd had been conditioned throughout his life never to give up, so he reasoned that if he moved quickly he might yet gain his childhood goal of being first, not on foot but in the air, at the North Pole. The meager military budgets of the postwar era did not encourage the navy to spend money on another polar attempt, but the service agreed to cooperate with aspiring Commander Byrd if he went outside for the financing. Here his experience in negotiating with highly placed Americans, aided by his family credentials, would help him in his pursuit of expedition money.

The persuasive Byrd, in a single interview, extracted $15,000 from Edsel Ford of the automotive empire and gained a like amount from John D. Rockefeller Jr., with others following. Byrd liked a new Loening military biplane amphibian, with a boat hull and wheels that recessed during water landings and cranked down for hard-surface operation. Though there were only three, Byrd

RICHARD BYRD AND FLOYD BENNETT MADE THE PERFECT TEAM FOR A NORTH POLE FLIGHT. *(Library of Congress)*

collected all of them for his 1925 polar expedition, and got his pick of navy support personnel, too.

Because Byrd planned to begin his flights at Etah, in the far northwest of Greenland, he had to go in with Donald MacMillan, who was also receiving navy cooperation—he was backed by the National Geographic Society—for a more southerly Greenland survey. Byrd was junior in command to MacMillan, but in his persuasive way he was able to try just about everything he planned.

What Byrd wanted—a round-trip to the Pole aboard one of the Loenings—was not publicized. The expedition prospectus limited their flights to searching for new islands north of the known ones. Byrd's scheme was to leapfrog this assignment by setting up a chain of fuel dumps leading northward to a point where, in a fuel-filled Loening, he could make a run to the North Pole and gather everlasting fame for the U.S. Navy and Lieutenant Commander Richard Byrd.

But these plans were thoroughly frustrated. Though it was August, gales and blizzards blew along the north Greenland coast. When occasionally the three aircraft flew northwest during the eighteen days the expedition ship dared to linger at weather-scourged Etah, the fliers saw the channels between the incredibly rugged, mountainous islands choked with shifting ice cakes, with no usable landing spots for bases.

In the savage weather of that Greenland "summer" Byrd had to strive just to fly. There was no way to attempt the North Pole. But Byrd proved himself a fearless leader anyway, for all of the flying out of Etah was heroic. Planes and personnel were the worse for wear but survived.

It was during the hard Greenland days that Byrd sized up Floyd Bennett and had him appointed his personal aide. Not an officer, Bennett was a career navy air machinist mate who combined high skills as an airplane mechanic with pilot duties. His assignment, before he was recommended for Byrd's polar expedition, was flying and maintaining the amphibian biplane a cruiser carried for flights at sea. This little reconnaissance aircraft was fired by catapult into flight and, after a risky ship-side landing on return, was hoisted back aboard—not a mission for amateurs.

Floyd Bennett's background was far removed from Byrd's. As a child, Floyd went to live with an uncle when his own family was too poor to keep him in the Adirondack Mountains of upstate New York. The quiet youth managed to gain an eighth-grade education. Afterward he worked a hard winter lumbering to save enough money to attend auto mechanic school. His natural abilities in automotive maintenance promoted him from chauffeur to garage management. When America entered World War I, Bennett joined the navy, where he became one of the relatively few enlisted men taught to fly.

Commander Byrd found in Bennett the perfect right-hand man and a loyal confidante. Of Bennett, Byrd said he was "a good pilot and one of the finest practical men in the Navy for handling an airplane's temperamental mechanisms, and above that a real man, fearless and true—one in a million."[2]

On the return voyage from Greenland, Byrd asked Bennett to go with him when he tried again for the polar prize in the spring. Byrd would get a new expedition together to go to Spitsbergen with a big airplane. Then it would be just Bennett piloting and Byrd navigating to the North Pole and glory.

The senior expeditioner, Donald MacMillan, reported that he believed the airplane was too frail a vehicle for the savage weather of the polar region; and this was obviously the view of Amundsen-Ellsworth too, who, coming back from their plane disaster, switched to a dirigible for their next attempt. So Byrd had a task in convincing the navy to associate itself with a second Byrd airplane flight plan. Even with the new expedition's cost coming from the outside, the admirals weren't anxious to be associated with a failure. It wasn't until February of 1926 that Commander Byrd wrung permission and six months leave for Bennett and himself.

Early on, Byrd and Bennett chose a reasonably priced secondhand Fokker trimotor airplane. Fokker was a Dutch company of fine reputation. Now, however, automaker Ford had an airplane division manufacturing its own trimotors. Back to Edsel Ford went Richard Byrd. He explained that he was too poor to afford the Ford plane, probably hoping Edsel would ask father Henry to donate one of his. This didn't happen, so the supersalesman naval flier got around Edsel by promis-

JOSEPHINE FORD WAS THE DAUGHTER OF EXPEDITION SPONSOR EDSEL FORD. (*Smithsonian Air and Space Museum*)

ing to name his Fokker "Josephine Ford," honoring the benefactor's daughter. He came away with a $20,000 check. The younger Rockefeller matched the amount, and other donors were tapped.

The expedition needed sea transportation, so Byrd went to the War Shipping Board, overseer of vessels left over from World War I, and managed to secure the thirty-five-hundred-ton *Chantier* for his expedition at the cost of one dollar. He still needed about fifty support personnel for the expedition, but how to meet that payroll? The commander wrote letters, and word got around. It was dull peacetime for the army and navy, and Byrd was going north to plant the American flag at the North Pole. Hundreds volunteered to serve without pay.

Commander Byrd was able to pick and choose, and in the main he sought out fresh, strong, adventure-seeking young men willing to do the expedition's heavy lifting, balanced by a dozen or so experienced sailors and craftsmen. The *Chantier* sailed April 5, 1926, on the long voyage to Spitsbergen. Most of the voyagers were landlubbers and seasickness overcame many of them. Just the same, food was cooked and dishes washed, the ship kept clean, the hand-fired boilers stoked. "The sons of millionaires were rated the same as the sons of plumbers."[3]

Those who shoveled coal in the bowels of the *Chantier* for five thousand miles needed particularly vivid imaginations to believe they were part of a high-flying, record-seeking adventure.

On April 29 the *Chantier* approached Spitsbergen, following the tail end of an arctic storm, and the expeditioners found the situation in King's Bay harbor not at all to their liking. Byrd had planned to use the bay ice as a runway, but a mild winter had not frozen it properly. The recent storm had filled King's Bay with mildly dangerous ice cakes. Meanwhile the small dock space was occupied by a Norwegian gunboat attached to the other expedition. When Byrd asked them to move so he could unload his plane, the Norwegians replied they couldn't. They were hurriedly repairing a failed boiler so that the vessel could be ready to accompany the dirigible *Norge* as a search-and-rescue guard. The *Norge* was expected from the south within the week. Nor would the Norwegian Navy allow their powerless ship to be pulled into the bay and helplessly endangered by floating ice. "In a few days" the Americans could have the dock to themselves.

But Commander Byrd didn't want to wait a few days. It would not be good enough just to fly successfully to the Pole in the wake of Amundsen-Ellsworth's dirigible. Byrd-Bennett *must* be first, because they were about $30,000 short in paying for their expedition. Byrd expected to make that up, and more, by selling article, book, and film rights, as well as by working the lecture circuit. But few would buy or listen if Byrd flew in second to the *Norge*.

Four lifeboats from the *Chantier* were lashed together at shipside and a platform spread above, overlapping the boats. The body of the *Josephine Ford* would be hoisted from the ship's hold onto the platform; next, the wing delicately delivered and attached. Then the unwieldy mass must be very carefully rowed a mile or so through a loose ice field to the shore. Before that, the rowers would have hacked out a six-hundred-foot ramp through the beach ice barrier rimming King's Bay. The Norwegians warned Byrd that stormy weather was seldom absent and might suddenly blow in to wreck the brave enterprise.

And that just about happened: The plane's fuselage was down on the raft, and the wing was up lying across the deck, when a furious squall burst in from the sea. Men flung themselves onto the wing, which stirred and lifted but did not go over the side. The sneaky squall fronted a steady gale that raged for twelve hours—a miserable stretch for the shifts of drenched and shivering men on the raft staving off ice attacks and listening apprehensively to the hum of the cables that attached the raft to the ship. If the cables snapped, there was nothing to prevent the raft from being dragged to destruction in the ice-filled harbor.

After the storm departed as suddenly as it began, the Fokker's wing was successfully attached and the makeshift barge began a very slow (because the rowers were inexperienced) journey toward the gap cut into the shore ice. Once a growler (small iceberg), with a diabolical puff of wind pushing it, sailed toward Byrd's "aircraft carrier." But the crew was ready, sending two men to intercept it and fasten dynamite to its flanks. The berg was blown to ice fragments. When at length the crew successfully reached the lip of the ramp, sailors watching from the Norwegian gunboat raised "a throaty cheer in appreciation of a task well done; and a moment later its musicians, hastily assembled, played the Star-spangled Banner."[4]

After mighty exertion, the *Josephine Ford* was pushed up from the beach and its wheels exchanged for skis. Richard Byrd visited Roald Amundsen hoping for cooperation and good advice. Had Amundsen and Ellsworth played hardball then, Byrd's expedition would have halted at the beach, for Amundsen had leased all the flat area fronting King's Bay. But Amundsen was a friendly rival and went out of his way to be helpful. The best terrain for a snowy airfield lay next to Amundsen's headquarters, and the veteran explorer urged Byrd to use it. He recommended the tramping technique to set in place a good runway.

ROWING THE *JOSEPHINE FORD* THROUGH A KING'S BAY FILLED WITH FLOATING ICE. *(Library of Congress Prints and Photographs Division)*

THE NORGE'S SPITSBERGEN HAVEN NEARS COMPLETION. BYRD'S SKI-MOUNTED TRIMOTOR IS AT RIGHT. *(Library of Congress Prints and Photographs Division)*

Yes, they were in a race, but Amundsen would not have it an ugly affair.

The Americans fully used the summer's twenty-two hours of daylight to get the big Fokker, forty-three feet long with a seventy-four-foot wingspan, ready. The plane rested on the snowy mantle, and JOSEPHINE FORD stood out in huge letters near the emblem of an American eagle perched atop the globe. On May 3 a test flight was attempted, but a twisted ski aborted the takeoff, and there was a near wreck a second time for the same reason. The expedition was now short of airplane skis, with no local replacements or suitable wood. Amundsen sent a young Norwegian aide, Bernt Balchen (who in future would fly Byrd to the South Pole), over to help Byrd's crew with their ski problem.

Oak lifeboat oars were skillfully reshaped in Amundsen's workshop to become airplane skis, and the American practice of waxing the ski surfaces with shoe polish was vastly improved upon by the Norwegian method of burning a mixture of paraffin and resin into the wood. Bennett was able to get off on their next try and flew for two hours, testing everything. Then the *Norge* arrived, needing an engine change before it could go on to Alaska.

Captain Umberto Nobile offered to speed up the *Norge*'s preparations, but Amundsen said, "We are not in a race with Byrd"[5] and "we will wait for our

[Alaska] weather."[6] Amundsen was the same when Byrd came to him and announced, "Gentlemen, tomorrow morning I am taking off and flying straight to the North Pole."

Amundsen fairly bored him with his eyes as he answered, "That is all right with us."[7]

Perhaps Amundsen was thinking of his own ambitious years as an explorer, when he had come to Antarctica late and beat the official expedition of Robert Scott to become the first man at the South Pole.

Still, Amundsen-Ellsworth had doubts that the ski-mounted trimotor, when weighted with sufficient gasoline to drive it to the Pole and back, would be able to get off in the primitive conditions. Just after noon on May 8 the *Josephine Ford* lumbered down the runway . . . and lumbered off the end of it into a large snowbank where the tail tilted high and engine sound ceased—the blackest moment of the Byrd expedition.

Bennett and Byrd leaped from the plane and frantically burrowed into the snow to find out what had happened to the undercarriage and propellers. What luck! The snow cushioned all, and the Fokker was able to taxi back to the starting place. Containers with three hundred gallons of extra fuel were off-loaded, as well as two hundred pounds of souvenirs placed aboard by expeditioners to become "over the North Pole" prizes. (But a well-hidden ukulele did make the trip.)

Then the Norwegians made a final suggestion: Schedule your takeoff for dawn, when the ice is hardest and its most slippery. That night Amundsen and Ellsworth awakened as the *Josephine Ford* taxied nearby and roared to a climax. With its tail first tied fast then cut loose for the speediest getaway—and still totaling ten thousand pounds—the plane hurtled along the icy runway. At the proper moment (12:37 A.M., May 9) Floyd Bennett lifted the trimotor in a magnificent curve to the north, and the plane rapidly became a Pole-seeking speck.

The usually terrible arctic weather calmed for Byrd this time. The air was nearly still on the northward trip, and the sun was constantly available as a navigation aid above the glaring whiteness of the monotonous, ridged ice desert below. The temperature inside the cabin was 0 degrees, but the pair were dressed for it. Nevertheless, Byrd suffered frostbite on his hand taking outside readings of wind drift. Besides his sextant and regular compasses, Byrd had the newly invented sun compass, "a kind of reversal of the sundial . . . time of day is known, and the shadow of the sun, when it bisects the hand of the 24-hour clock, indicates the direction . . ."[8]

Engine noise forced the two to communicate by writing, and Byrd passed a stream of course-correction notes up to pilot Bennett. The navigator was also taken up with the math of fuel consumption. The flight continued to be routine until an hour below the Pole when the right engine began throwing oil. Bennett wanted to seek a landing spot to repair the leak, warning if they did not "that motor will stop."[9] But they were so close to the prize, Byrd risked all to go for it. Oil kept oozing, but pressure showed normal and the motor ran as before.

At 9:02 A.M. Byrd gleefully shook Bennett's hand, informing the pilot that the *Josephine Ford* was at the Pole. As the trimotor circled thirteen times, Byrd snapped photographs of polar ice pack similar to what the fliers had been viewing for hours. Byrd did not drop an American flag, remarking that Peary had already planted the Stars and Stripes. Then, as the plane banked onto its return course, Byrd's sextant slid and broke on the floor. They wouldn't know *where* they were, but in perfect weather with the sun compass they could compute a "dead reckoning" course in the exact *direction* of Spitsbergen.

BYRD USED HIS SUN COMPASS FOR "DEAD RECKONING" NAVIGATION AFTER HIS SEXTANT BROKE. (*Library of Congress*)

Neither was particularly worried; indeed, both slipped into postvictory lassitude. Byrd had briefly relieved Bennett at the controls all along, but they switched more often on the return because each was fighting drowsiness. After a while the oil leak stopped when the oil level lowered below the hole of the popped rivet. The navigator was sure they were on the line to Spitsbergen. Perhaps the flight verged toward boredom as they anticipated the delights of fame to come.

At King's Bay, in Amundsen's camp, the dinner talk was all about Byrd. Outside of normal human concerns, they were anxious to see the Fokker trimotor again. For if Byrd disappeared, they would use the *Norge* for an air search, which, if it turned out to be lengthy, would ruin their own expedition goals. They were surprised when they heard the airplane motor droning into a landing approach—for it was hours earlier than expected—but filled with joyful relief. The *Norge* men rushed forth to greet the new polar heroes. The Byrd party, also surprised by the early return, were outrun. It was Amundsen who as first greeter

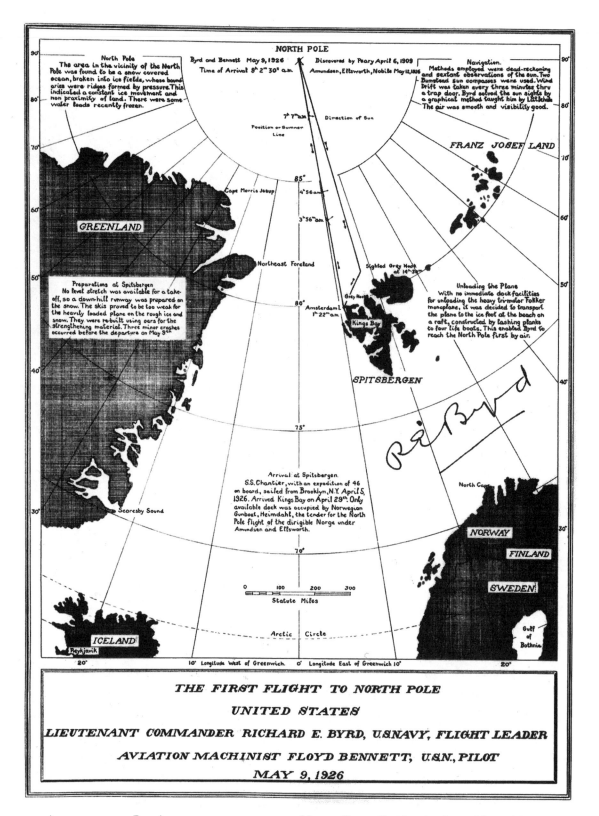

NORTH POLE

Byrd and Bennett May 9, 1926
Time of Arrival 8ʰ 2ᵐ 30ˢ a.m.

Discovered by Peary April 6, 1909
Amundsen, Ellsworth, Nobile May 12,1926

North Pole
The area in the vicinity of the North Pole was found to be a snow covered ocean, broken into ice fields, whose boundaries were ridges formed by pressure. This indicated a constant ice movement and non proximity of land. There were some water leads recently frozen.

Navigation.
Methods employed were dead-reckoning and sextant observations of the sun. Two Bumstead sun compasses were used. Wind Drift was taken every three minutes thru a trap door. Byrd solved the sun sights by a graphical method taught him by Littlehales. The air was smooth and visibility good.

7ʰ 7ᵐ a.m. — Direction of Sun

Position or Sumner Line

FRANZ JOSEF LAND

Cape Morris Jesup

85°

4ʰ 56ᵐ a.m.

3ʰ 56ᵐ a.m.

GREENLAND

Northeast Foreland

Sighted Grey Hook at 14ʰ

Preparations at Spitsbergen
No level stretch was available for a take-off, so a down-hill runway was prepared on the snow. The skis proved to be too weak for the heavily loaded plane on the rough ice and snow. They were re-built using oars for the strengthening material. Three minor crashes occurred before the departure on May 9ᵗʰ.

80°

Amsterdam I.
1ʰ 22ᵐ a.m.

Grey Hook

Kings Bay

Unloading the Plane
With no immediate dock facilities for unloading the heavy tri-motor Fokker monoplane, it was decided to transport the plane to the ice foot at the beach on a raft, constructed by lashing planks to four life boats. This enabled Byrd to reach the North Pole first by air.

SPITSBERGEN

75°

R E Byrd

North Cape

Arrival at Spitsbergen.
S.S. Chantier, with an expedition of 46 on board, sailed from Brooklyn, N.Y. April 5, 1926. Arrived Kings Bay on April 29ᵗʰ. Only available dock was occupied by Norwegian Gunboat, Heimdahl, the tender for the North Pole flight of the dirigible Norge under Amundsen and Ellsworth.

Scoresby Sound

70°

NORWAY

FINLAND

SWEDEN

0   100   200   300
Statute Miles

Arctic Circle

ICELAND
Reykjavik

Gulf of Bothnia

20°   10° Longitude West of Greenwich.   0°   Longitude East of Greenwich 10°   20°

THE FIRST FLIGHT TO NORTH POLE
UNITED STATES
LIEUTENANT COMMANDER RICHARD E. BYRD, U.S. NAVY, FLIGHT LEADER
AVIATION MACHINIST FLOYD BENNETT, U.S.N., PILOT
MAY 9, 1926

A MAP SHOWING BYRD'S CLAIMED FLIGHT TO THE NORTH POLE. *(Smithsonian Air and Space Museum)* soundly kissed Byrd and Bennett.

Why were they early? Byrd responded that they had a light tailwind going up and a strong one hastening their return. The Byrd and Bennett flight to and from the North Pole in fifteen and one half hours was certified into the record book by the National Geographic Society. Ahead in America lay adulation and bestowed honors, most prominently the award to both fliers of the Congressional Medal of Honor. Yet in Europe there was doubt of the accomplishment, sour grapes or otherwise.

How fast could the Fokker trimotor fly? Byrd claimed a normal 100 miles per hour and top speed of 120 miles per hour. Critics think it was

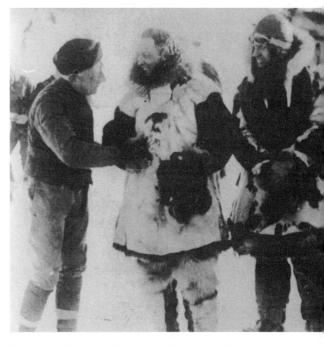

AMUNDSEN GREETS BYRD AND BENNETT. THEIR RETURN RELIEVED NORGE OF AIR-SEARCH RESPONSIBILITY. *(Smithsonian Air and Space Museum)*

more like 85 miles per hour. Studies of 1926 weather maps, prepared hundreds or thousands of miles distant from the North Pole, led a critic to claim in 1959 that arctic tailwinds were unlikely during Byrd's flight. In 1996, in America, researchers who studied air navigation computations handwritten by Byrd on the historic flight concluded that the fliers did not reach the North Pole before turning back.

Scientific scholars weren't greatly impressed by the Byrd-Bennett feat. Ocean depth soundings made by Amundsen and Ellsworth on the ice pack the previous year already certified that no land lay underneath the Pole. One arctic historian, Jeanette Mirsky, in a survey volume of polar exploration awards Byrd and Bennett but three lines.

But they were polar heroes in the realm of popular fame and set the tone for many future record-seeking flights in the twenties and thirties. Floyd Bennett died two years later of pneumonia aggravated by participation in a heroic search-and-rescue operation. Richard Byrd, though, went forward to become the last great popular explorer with a series of expeditions to Antarctica, during which he was first to fly over the South Pole (1928).

CHAPTER SIX

TRIUMPH OF THE *NORGE*

WHEN RIISER-LARSEN WAS IN ITALY BUYING THE TWO
Dornier Wals for the first expedition, he learned that Italy had a dirigible capa-
ble of polar flight available at a good price. In the twenties the Italian govern-
ment had an aeronautical factory producing small dirigibles for its armed forces.
They sold abroad, too, and Japan and the United States were customers. The
motivation behind the good price was political. Benito Mussolini had raised the
Fascist party to power, and the national mood was ultrapatriotic. An Italian-made,
Italian-crewed dirigible over the North Pole would be good publicity for the
Fascist dictatorship to come.

In May and June of 1925 Amundsen, Ellsworth, and company had had twenty-
five days of ice-pack imprisonment to think about the advantages of a dirigible
over an airplane as a vehicle of polar exploration. They decided to obtain one,
should they be fortunate enough to escape. Already, on July 15, just ten days after
the expedition's triumphal royal reception at Oslo, the Italians received a
telegram from Amundsen opening negotiations for their dirigible.

Colonel Umberto Nobile came up to Oslo empowered by Mussolini to make
the best deal possible with the famed Norwegian explorer. Nobile was both
superintendent at the aeronautical factory and its chief dirigible designer. The
Italian preferred to plan and build a special airship for polar flight. But if

Amundsen were in a hurry, they also had a two-year-old, serviceable army dirigible that could be modified. The important thing was to get Italy into the arctic, and the headlines, by carrying along a famous explorer.

Amundsen and Ellsworth *were* in a hurry. They hoped to fly over the North Pole to Alaska the next spring. Nobile led off with a free deal: Mussolini would donate the *N-1* army dirigible for use on the polar flight provided it was crewed by Italians and carried the Italian flag, with Amundsen and Ellsworth as guest explorers.

Absolutely not! The proud Norwegian despised the idea of sharing expedition authority. He had not before and would not now, even in this unfamiliar aerial era. It was going to be a Norwegian-American, Amundsen and Ellsworth expedition—period. They wanted to buy an airship, rename it *Norge* (Norway), crew it predominantly with Norwegians, and fly the national flag. Amundsen was uncompromising.

The aristocratic Italian colonel smoothly shifted gears. The government would sell the dirigible *N-1* to the expedition for $75,000. Furthermore, if the airship remained in acceptable condition, Italy would buy it back for $46,000. Thus in ideal circumstances the use-lease would cost only $29,000. Ellsworth had been ready to go as high as $100,000. What a deal! However, Amundsen and Ellsworth would have to accept at least five Italian crew members. They did, and took Nobile, too, as airship commander, reasoning that, as its designer, he knew the most about their *Norge*.

Then followed a tense exchange in defining the limits of control of the "airship commander," with Amundsen emphasizing its "hired pilot" aspect and Nobile trying to keep as much power as possible: If, when they reached the Pole, Nobile wanted for sound technical reasons to turn back to King's Bay, would he have the authority? *No,* declared the veteran explorer.

Nobile backed down: Would you respectfully consider my opinion? *Of course,* snapped Amundsen.

The deal was struck, but Amundsen saw Nobile solely as a dirigible driver, while the proud Italian looked down on Amundsen and Ellsworth as useless (unless the party went down on the ice pack) and underfoot passengers. Unsurprisingly, these attitudes eventually caused unbecoming publicity.

Amundsen then went off to America to lecture, while Ellsworth settled his father's estate. The Norwegian Aero Club was again administering the expedition, and in negotiating details of the contract with them, Nobile made good Italian progress. When Amundsen and Ellsworth went to Rome to officially

WALKING THE *NORGE* INSIDE. *(Library of Congress)*

receive the *Norge* from Mussolini, they learned that the Aero Club had agreed to enlarge the expedition title to Amundsen-Ellsworth-Nobile—and there were other contract favors to him, including a hefty salary hike. Then Amundsen and Ellsworth (leaving Riiser-Larsen on the airship as second in command) sailed to Spitsbergen to prepare the expedition base.

The *Norge* departed Rome April 10, 1926. Flying via the English airship station at Pulham to Oslo, and on to Leningrad (now Saint Petersburg, Russia), they then waited until May 5 for completion of the King's Bay facility, which a snowy spring had delayed. Adding on the final leg of the journey from Vadsö, in furthest north Norway, to Spitsbergen, the *Norge* had flown about four thousand miles from Rome. Surely this was a thorough shakedown voyage for the joint Italian-Scandinavian crew, and a generally harmonious one, too.

At King's Bay the landing was accomplished smoothly by carefully letting down the airship to a level where ropes could be hurled to ground personnel. They pulled the *Norge* down to nearly head level and then walked it into its snug canvas-covered shelter. After what they had been through already during the 103 hours it had taken to fly from Rome, the North Pole did not seem, at less than 800 miles, so far off for the confident crew.

The *Norge* was a small dirigible (some German airships were several times larger) 348 feet long, weighing about 20 tons, and refitted for a 3,500-mile fuel range (the polar flight was expected to be about 2,500 miles). Three Mayback engines of 250 horsepower housed in enclosures that could accommodate a mechanic as well, could push the *Norge* at a lean cruising speed of 50 miles per hour. The motors were slung beneath the gasbag in a triangular position. The rear-point engine ran always, while the widely separated ones beneath the center section alternated running time in ordinary flight.

The small, crowded main gondola beneath the dirigible's belly was bare and open at the top (no heat), with a ladder to climb to the main keel pathway. This ran the length of the airship below the gas cells, with feeder aisles to the engine enclosures and other ladders amid the hydrogen-filled sacks—even leading to the top of the *Norge* where one could take a stroll. Along the keel were stored all of the emergency supplies for postcrash-living on the ice pack. This was a flaw, for it was likely in such an accident that the gasbag would tear away from the gondola and carry off their life-sustaining gear.

The *Norge* was crewed north of Spitsbergen by the airship commander, a full-time navigator and an assistant who steered, a helmsman controlling the elevators, six engine-mechanic–airship riggers, two radio experts to operate the 1,000-mile-range Marconi radio, and a meteorologist. Six Italians, six Norwegians, and one Swede. Additionally, it carried two explorers and a jour-

SAYING GOOD-BYE. *(Library of Congress)*

nalist, plus "the only female aboard," twelve-pound Titina, Nobile's adored pet terrier.

The departure of the *Norge*, at 8:55 A.M. on May 11, was magnificent. So smooth and even was the liftoff that it seemed to Ellsworth:

> We were not rising; we were poised, and the world was falling away from us as if lowered by hydraulic power. The walls of the fjord leisurely went downward past us. Familiar faces, uplifted toward us, grew indistinct and then unrecognizable.
>
> Swarms of gulls and other polar birds flew out of their rookeries in the cliffs to inspect this huge new cousin of the air. The air vibrated with thousands of flashing wings and shrill, excited cries. In the stillness of our cabin we could hear the roaring of the *Josephine Ford* far below, as Byrd and Floyd Bennett took off to bear us company during the first stage of our journey.[1]

Then engines were started, and the dirigible moved off north at fifty miles per hour in perfect sunny weather, with the faster Fokker flying rings around it for the first hour, then dipping wings in salute and turning back. The *Norge* passed over the Edge just north of Spitsbergen and cruised majestically above the glaring, sterile ice desert, where soon the airship's stout shadow became the sole movement below.

When the dirigible reached 87°44' north, Nobile cut speed, descending to a few hundred feet altitude, and Amundsen, Ellsworth, Riiser-Larsen, and Omdal gathered in the gondola to survey the icescape of their former prison. All agreed they were pleased to be on an airship in these parts instead of an airplane.

Not that they were traveling deluxe: The frigid, canvas-covered basketwork cabin was just thirty feet by six, and in its three cubbyholes, ten persons, including the outsize egos of Amundsen and Nobile, and a little dog were crowded together for three mainly sleepless days. According to Amundsen:

> There was simply no room for quarreling. A certain amount of elbow-room is required for exhibitions of temper . . . a more peaceful and tranquil spot than the *Norge* during the flight has never existed . . . we never heard an angry word nor saw an unpleasant expression during the whole flight.[2]

By oversight they had left their water supply behind, but aboard the *Norge* it would not have remained liquid a half hour after departure. The same frozen fate occurred with the packed lunches—the eggs became as solid as cue balls. The travelers subsisted on the stew in numerous thermos jugs.

At twelve hours out, approaching 88° north, a massive fog bank loomed, and once they were in it, ice started to sheathe the *Norge*'s bulk, adding weight and masking the gondola windows. Already the airship had had temporary engine failure because of icing in the carburetor intake. To get out of the icy cloud, Nobile climbed from eighteen hundred to thirty-one hundred feet where the *Norge* broke into sunshine that melted the ice. Fortunately, by the time the expedition cruised near the North Pole, clear weather prevailed again.

As Nobile slid the dirigible downward to three hundred feet, navigator Riiser-Larsen knelt, sighting the sun in his sextant, and when the orb's image covered the bubble reg-

COLONEL NOBILE TREADS THE NARROW KEEL OF THE *NORGE*. NOTE THE STORAGE OF SURVIVAL ITEMS IN THE AIRSHIP'S RIGGING. *(Library of Congress Prints and Photographs Division)*

ister exactly, he cried out, "Here we are!" Engines idled and the *Norge* hung peacefully above the North Pole, sixteen and one-half hours out of King's Bay, 1:25 A.M., May 12. Word of the expedition's first triumph crackled out by radio to the world. The national flags of Norway, the United States, and Italy, tipped with leaded darts, descended and successfully stuck into the snow. The Italian flag was by far the largest. It had flown at the stern of *N-1* before it became *Norge* and its nationality changed.

Here, a double historical precedent was set aboard the *Norge*. Amundsen had installed an old comrade, Oscar Wisting, as helmsman. He had stood beside Amundsen at the planting of the Norwegian flag on the South Pole fifteen years ago. Now over the North Pole the two veterans clasped hands in silent pathos as the only two men who had achieved both Poles.

AMUNDSEN, THE PASSENGER, HAD NO AIRBORNE DUTIES. *(Library of Congress Prints and Photographs Division)*

Pushed by a favorable breeze, the *Norge* moved forward over the last broad unknown area on the roof of the globe. It was probably all more ice pack, yet there was room for a huge undiscovered island. They proceeded, scanning a visual circumference of about fifty miles, navigating over the unknown—when someone reported a mountain on the horizon! The dirigible turned, but seemed to make no progress toward the fascinating vision. "It's just a Cape Flyaway," announced Amundsen as the arctic mirage faded into nothingness.[3]

Five-and-a-half hours past the North Pole they crossed the "Ice Pole" at the center of the arctic ocean and its permanent ice pack. Looking down, Ellsworth saw it as a "chaos of barricades and ridges," perhaps the result of centrifugal compression by Arctic Ocean currents.[4] The airborne pioneers hadn't seen a sign of any animal life but their own since just beyond the Edge. But here at 86° north they were surprised by "One lone polar bear track. What a mockery to our egotism!" wrote Ellsworth, remembering. "Yet there it was, plainly crossing a large ice floe . . . something alive and seeking, like ourselves."[5]

Then, barring the way to Alaska, fog banks loomed and soon overcast all. The weather was gathering to fight them till the end. Though the soggy areas were intermittent, it sometimes took an hour to penetrate the overcast, and serious icing affected all surfaces of the dirigible. Nobile consulted with the meteorologist, Swede Finn Malmgren, who constantly analyzed water content in the mists and advised the best altitudes. The clammy moisture invaded the semi-open cabin.

Ice accumulation weighted the *Norge*'s nose. Fuel and ballast were moved back to rebalance the airship, for if the condition worsened, the nose-heavy craft would plunge into the ice. Frost and icicles thickened and covered outside instruments. The radiomen kept losing the long, trailing antenna, which had become an awkward 450-foot icicle. Because of distance, and now radio malfunction, the world had not heard from the *Norge* for many hours.

The most nerve-racking phenomenon was the release of ice pieces, perhaps from quivering guy wires, that fell into the propeller arcs and were thrown back to strike all along the *Norge's* underside with the sound of pistol shots causing holes and tears. The riggers roamed repairing the fabric with rubber cement until the adhesive was all used up. If these random projectiles ever punctured gas sacks, they'd be finished! The sixteen, plus dog, endured hours of possible instant destruction by these ice missiles. As uncovered punctures accumulated, a braying sound arose, ranging in tones from trumpets to sirens as the wind blasted through. But the gas sacks remained safe.

Riiser-Larsen's navigation had to be partly by instinct, for he had only one more sun shot. Then, finally, the ice-jittered fliers were roused by the navigator's land cry—forty-seven hours and two thousand miles out of Spitsbergen. As they rode back over the Edge, coming in as planned past Point Barrow, Alaska, the icing ceased. A radio message flashed south that the *Norge* had been glimpsed amid fog, snow, and scudding cloud.

The expedition was sorely in need of new and accurate weather information. Had their radio been working they would have verified that a deep, swirling low-pressure system stretched to the west over the Bering Sea, while in central Alaska a placid, clear, high-pressure area lay over Fairbanks. Nome, on the Bering Sea, was their planned destination, and Nobile and Malmgrem opted to feel their way west along the coast until weather improvement allowed them to make a left turn south, straight across the mountains to Nome. Pushed by tailwinds, the *Norge* went into the storm.

The airship now flew west at very low altitudes to maintain visual contact with the terrain and its contours. The village of Wainwright appeared, and the *Norge* flew over the house where Amundsen and Omdal had lived three years earlier when they tried to fly out from Alaska. They were bowled along westward in a rising gale as a short Alaskan night, more a deep twilight, came on.

After the trailing radio antenna banged on a half-seen hilltop, Nobile ordered a rise to about thirty-five hundred feet, as high as he dared in the storm. For an hour or more the howling nor'easter hurled them ahead in blind flight. Finally in morning light they began to clear the cloud tops. The radiomen cleaned their antenna of ice and, though unable to send, received a strong signal—Nome—to the southeast. Riiser-Larsen climbed through the gas cells and took a bumpy sun shot *atop* the rocking dirigible. It was agreed they were nearly over Siberia, so the *Norge* turned back into the wind with three motors straining to seek Alaska again.

They had to fly low for safety when they reached the coast, because descent straight down would be through blinding fog. They first saw ice pack, then crossed the stormy open sea somewhere north of the Bering Strait. Nobile now moved to hands-on operation of airship controls. *Norge* had been sixty-plus hours in the air when, bucking the bumps at an altitude of 150 feet, they at length approached Alaska's cloud-choked western coast. Where, they could not say.

Providentially, their landfall was over a village, but there was dispute as to which it might be. Amundsen thought it was Kivalina, and Omdal excitedly agreed, pointing out a landmark: the anvil-shaped mountain nearby! But no one else saw such a mountain. Omdal's fatigue had made him hallucinate. They decided to go up through the fog to the sun above it and make a sextant verification of position.

They emerged into sunshine at about four thousand feet. The solar heat expanded the volatile hydrogen gas inside the bags. This gave more lift against the decreased outside air pressure. If unchecked this would have ended in an explosion. With the nose rising now beyond elevator control, Nobile screamed in English at two Norwegians to join others running to the nose to weight it back down into control. They just stared. He screamed again, relapsing into Italian from English, and in delayed reaction they raced forward. Down came the nose at fifty-four hundred feet and soon there was a scramble to the rear to rebalance, so the *Norge* was saved.

Fortunately, the navigator got his sun shot and verified they were over Kivalina, about 240 miles above Nome. Nobile advised not to try a difficult landing there, and his view was accepted. The *Norge* was fueled for at least seven more hours, and he wanted to reach Nome. Though it mattered little to Amundsen and Ellsworth where in Alaska they disembarked, Nobile had Mussolini and strong aviation rivals in Italy looking over his shoulder.

THE PERFECT LANDING AT TELLER, ALASKA. *(Library of Congress Prints and Photographs Division)*

The Seward Peninsula, with interior mountains rising to nearly

Peacemaker Ellsworth sits between prima donnas Amundsen and Nobile. Riiser-Larsen is at far left. Above Amundsen is Oscar Wisting, who was with Amundsen at the South Pole. *(Smithsonian Air and Space Museum)*

four thousand feet, barred direct approach to Nome. Instead they had to follow, below the soup, the coastline around the peninsula. Their early course lay southwest till the turn at Cape Prince of Wales on Bering Strait, and a tailwind of sixty miles per hour really moved them along. If their extraordinary engines ever failed, *Norge* would be helplessly bowled across to somewhere in wildest Siberia. Nobile stationed Riiser-Larsen, leaning forward from a porthole, to shout if he saw something ahead higher than the airship.

So they rounded the cape and then labored in a sidewind. Almost seventy hours! All the crew staggered under fatigue—and so the call now for third engine start-up was not immediately answered. The mechanic was not asleep, but sheer exhaustion slowed his reaction time.

Two more hours, then beneath the streaming scud they spotted a three-masted ship canted into shore ice. Beyond they saw a row of houses. Hearts leaped for joy: Nome! But flying over showed them nothing more than that thin strip of buildings. Not Nome . . . and disappointment dragged off their remaining resolve.

The shore ice appeared smooth, and sufficient manpower came forward from the village below to aid them. (Riiser-Larsen hallucinated a unit of "cavalry" out of a line of shore rocks.) They decided, despite the wind, to land at this unknown place. Riiser-Larsen proposed that they break out the canvas sides of the cabin to allow everyone to leave at the same time. Nobile opposed this, for it meant losing the airship to the elements. Amundsen decided to back Nobile in a by-the-book landing. A weighted dragline was let down and lines were thrown over as the dirigible slowly approached the steadfast villagers. Near the surface a most welcome calm occurred (a miracle, Amundsen believed). The lines were grasped, and the *Norge* was safely down, seventy-one hours out of King's Bay, Spitsbergen.

Nobile enforced precedence: Amundsen and Ellsworth went first, then others, as he and the riggers pulled the toggles venting the gas sacks. Soon the airship would resemble a crumpled handkerchief. Nobile and Titina stepped off last. The little dog frolicked in the snow; Titina had been an exemplary transpolar passenger and had only moaned in times of extreme human distress.

Amundsen dazedly asked what place this was. Teller. Teller, of course. He and Ellsworth staggered toward the thin line of houses that contained food and beds. The fifty or so predominantly Eskimo residents of Teller handled the *Norge* and its men as if they were used to having transpolar dirigibles drop in on them. Seventy miles southeast in Nome there was deep chagrin.

Teller had an unused wireless office that the *Norge*'s radiomen quickly repaired to connect them to the outside world. Amundsen and Ellsworth had made an exclusive contract with the *New York Times* for expedition publicity. To their irritation, however, Nobile was sending his own stories wherever he pleased, fulfilling Mussolini's intent to emphasize the Italian nature of the transpolar conquest. The expedition leaders had not noticed the change approving this that Nobile had negotiated into his contract.

Nobile and his Italians remained at Teller for eighteen days dismantling and packing the *Norge* for shipment. (The Italian government did buy back the airship.) There was no hurry, for no one could leave Alaska until, in about a month, the first ship of the season came up to Nome. Amundsen and Ellsworth, however, went down to Nome by dogsled. The great explorer had truly enjoyed the parades and the acclaim from the crowds when he had come in from an expedition to some piece of the unknown. Nome had feted him in the past, and he looked for more.

This vanity was punctured. The town had prepared itself as the end partner of "Rome to Nome." Amundsen had failed them by landing the historic flight in obscure Teller. So no parade; nothing was done. Just a few old friends welcomed

Roald Amundsen. And he had to stay a month in the place! When Nobile came to Nome later, he brought a special gift and blessing from the Pope. Nome's priest was Italian, so special attention was given to Nobile and parties were held for him and his men, which made the proud Norwegian jealous.

Another grievance was that Nobile had severely limited the Norwegian contingents' baggage. Therefore, they remained plainly dressed when they arrived at Seattle. The sizable Italian colony there had been mobilized and came out in chartered boats to surround the steamer. When Nobile appeared on deck to bestow the Fascist salute on his cheering admirers, he cut a splendid figure in full officer's uniform. Amundsen was angered by the display of a double standard.

Unfortunately, he chose to make public his anger with "hired pilot" Nobile and told of instances when the airship commander may have guided the *Norge* in a slipshod and dangerous way. Nobile replied, of course, and emphasized the do-nothing, know-nothing aspects of Amundsen and Ellsworth aboard the *Norge*. Of Ellsworth, who in his mild manner had tried to mediate between the prima donnas, Nobile wrote dismissively: "Mr. Ellsworth on our expedition was just a passenger whom I took on board at Spitsbergen and left at Teller."

Such pettiness did not detract from the historic and heroic character of the *Norge*'s triumph. They had bisected with "a line of light" the dark unknown at the center of the Arctic Ocean, settling the age-old question of whether any landmass capped the top of the world. In a small dirigible built for flight in sunny Mediterranean skies, the expedition had flown from Rome to the Pacific Ocean, 7,800 miles in 171 hours. It was a great, fortunate, personal triumph for airship commander Umberto Nobile, one he might have left well enough alone.

CHAPTER SEVEN

WILKINS AND EIELSON: MEANT FOR EACH OTHER

"SOME MEN SEE THINGS AS THEY ARE AND SAY—WHY? Others dream things that never were and say—why not?" wrote Aeschylus of Athens, circa 500 B.C.

George Hubert Wilkins started life on an isolated sheep ranch in Australia, but ambitious curiosity and an instinct to follow up "things that never were" soon set his feet into seven-league boots of destiny.

Wilkins was born thirteenth and last into his family in 1888; his parents had retired to the city of Adelaide by the time he reached his teens. An interest in mechanics led young Wilkins to university engineering classes, which he paid for by working as an electrician. He was installing wiring in an Adelaide theater when it happened that a tent carnival, including a primitive motion picture show, was setting up nearby. The operators were having trouble with their generator until Wilkins got it going. They in turn satisfied his curiosity about the new craft and art of movie making. Wilkins was fascinated, and when the show left town he went with them.

Applying his bold genius to the new medium, the lad progressed quickly from projectionist to cameraman, and on to writing and directing movies of that early time. Indeed, Wilkins's reputation spread to faraway England, from where a top-notch job offer came in 1908, when he was twenty.

While making farewells in Adelaide, he was suddenly inspired to stow away on a ship going over to nearby Sydney. Perhaps this experience could be converted into a movie plot that he could present to his English employer. But it happened that Wilkins erred in choosing his ship. Discovered early on—and beaten up for his cheek—the stowaway learned that this vessel's first port of call would be in Africa! Many weeks later, after the ship captain was thoroughly satisfied Wilkins had worked out his passage, he was put ashore in the colorful, mysterious port of Algiers.

There he fell in with an Italian spy's amateurish attempt at North African espionage, which ended with the young Australian being carried off by camel caravan to be sold at some desert slave market. It happened, though, that an Arab girl was smitten with Wilkins and helped him escape to make his way to London, where his new job opened the door to a decade and more of adventure.

Wilkins was attracted to aeronautics—then, like the movies, in its early experimental phase. He claimed a first in aerial movie filming when, perched on a bicycle seat attached to the airplane's nose, he filmed—at nearly ground level—a hare bounding ahead of mounted huntsmen. He also went ballooning to film Santa Claus parachuting into London. But after Santa's departure, the balloon controls jammed. For a day and a half the runaway gasbag careened over Britain and the North Sea, causing acute discomfort to its passengers before descending roughly—fortunately, on land. Not daunted, Wilkins had learned to fly by 1912.

The young man went to the Balkans to become the first war cinematographer as he covered a conflict between Turkey and Bulgaria. Back in England, he applied to be filmmaker on an antarctic expedition but was sent instead on the Canadian arctic expedition of Vilhjalmur Stefansson. Wilkins soon rose to second-in-command in supply support of the explorer's expeditions to map the northernmost arctic islands and look for others. In the years he was with him, Wilkins estimated he must have slogged along for five thousand miles. Stefansson recalled that his assistant spent much time telling him about how much more efficient it would be to *fly over* the polar wastes.

Stefansson, an Icelandic American from North Dakota, studied the Eskimo way of survival and managed to stay north of the Arctic Circle for five years.

G. H. WILKINS, AUSTRALIAN ADVENTURER.

(Smithsonian Air and Space Museum)

Wilkins quit after three to go to the action of World War I and became Australia's finest war photographer. His daring forays to film at the front lines caused Australia's commanding general to comment that Captain Wilkins was the bravest Aussie of all.

Postwar, in 1919, Wilkins sought to return to the arctic on his terms. He tried to obtain a war-surplus dirigible for polar exploration. Both the British and the Germans declined, the latter fearing to risk their zeppelins' reputation in another fiasco like Wellman's.

Instead Wilkins gained financial backing so that he could compete in the great Europe-to-Australia air derby. His plane, however, crash-landed on the Mediterranean island of Crete. There was also an adventure into Communist Russia with an American film actress, a survey of the fringe of Antarctica, and a scientific expedition among Aborigines in the jungles of north Australia.

This slim, balding man, who owned such an unmatchable résumé in twentieth-century adventuring, did not impress others as a swashbuckling, romantic, devil-may-care individual. When in the civilized world, Captain Wilkins seemed a formal, often silent individual, who withheld his inquisitive personality from exhibition. But his record in pushing beyond the limits of available technology, his personal bravery and unfailing knack of good luck, continued to provide him with backers for each new project.

In 1925, on the heels of Amundsen's failed attempt to reach the North Pole in the Dorniers, an American news service approached Wilkins about backing him in a transpolar flight from Alaska. Flying the arctic was a goal at the top of the Australian's list, so he went to America, where further support came from a Detroit newspaper and rich men of the auto industry. Suddenly Captain Wilkins had more than he wanted: three new airplanes, pilots on leave from a Michigan army air base, support personnel, reporters. Because Wilkins wanted a Byrd-like role as flight director and air navigator, he needed a personal pilot who would be nearest to an extension of himself. His arctic mentor Stefansson recommended a fellow North Dakotan, Ben Eielson.

Carl Ben Eielson, born 1897 in the village of Hatton, North Dakota, came into the Army Air Service among the youngest batch of volunteers for pilot training in World War I. And he was one of the many who had not seen combat by the time the war ended. Eielson's father, owner of Hatton's general store, expected his son to return to law school. Ben tried, but flying's allure soon prompted him, with the excuse of earning money for law studies, to obtain a war-surplus "Jenny" biplane and become a typical gypsy pilot or barnstormer, roaming the Great Plains in summer, attracting crowds by stunting, and then carrying passengers aloft for fun and profit.

Like Lincoln Ellsworth's father, Mr. Ole Eielson Sr. was passionately opposed to Ben's flying because he feared this son would surely kill himself. From his childhood, Ben had been a persistent sleepwalker, and now when, as a barnstorming pilot, he visited Hatton, he relived his flights in a family bedroom. Past midnight he leaped out of bed, took his cockpit seat by sliding backward onto a chair, and grasped a splat in its back as his Jenny's "stick." With sweating face, moans, and cries, Ben dramatized by word and motion the despair of a flier nearly out of gas and fumbling blindly for a nighttime landing. Finally he sighed, said "landed safely!", awakened, and crawled back into bed.[1]

Near the end of that glorious, free-flying summer of 1920, Ben did wrap Jenny's wing around a telegraph pole. It might be possible to repair the plane, but . . . Ben gave in to the pleas of his father,

A GLAMOROUS PORTRAIT OF CARL BEN EIELSON. *(Smithsonian Air and Space Museum)*

brothers, and sisters. It did make better sense to be a "live lawyer instead of a dead pilot." After Ben graduated from the University of North Dakota, Ole Eielson sent his son to the urban east, far from summer flying, to finish law training in Washington, DC.

Ben got a guard job at the Capitol to help pay for his schooling. He became friendly with the delegate from the Territory of Alaska, who practiced his lobbying technique on Eielson. Alaska was "the great land," the last American frontier, a beckoning, still-empty land of opportunity! Ben listened and remembered one fact: Though the U.S. Army Air Service had flown four planes to Alaska and back the past summer, there were currently *no airplanes* in Alaska. Via his friend, Eielson was able to obtain a job in Alaska teaching high school in the main inland town of Fairbanks.

Eielson then went back to Hatton and told his dad that he just couldn't stick with the law, and that he'd gotten a teaching job in Alaska. Well, Ole's parents reasoned they had brought him across the sea from Norway, all the way to North Dakota, and now he was moving on to the far northern frontier. That was destiny right and proper, and there were *no airplanes* in Alaska.

Teacher Ben Eielson spent as much time talking up flying in Alaska as he did leading English class or coaching basketball. Certainly the territory needed a swifter means of transport than dog teams and canoes. A railroad had poked up through the mountains from the seaport of Anchorage, but there was scarcely a dirt road outside of Fairbanks in a basin covering thousands of square miles. The opportunity for moving people and equipment was everywhere. Why not *fly them?* Ben had no money and couldn't ask his father for funds, but a Fairbanks syndicate soon formed, and one day, in 1923, the railroad delivered a boxed Jenny airplane that Eielson assembled.

Betting among townfolk ran heavily against "the flying professor" getting into the sky, for this was Alaska, rough and tough. But Ben easily lifted Jenny off the former racetrack, climbed high, allowed the plane to fall into a spin—a thrill for onlookers expecting a crash—and then pulled out and landed. That morning Ben had been a crackpot; now, in the evening, he was a hero.

The next summer was spent roaming over the central Alaskan wilderness, which was broken here and there by a village, a mine, a trapper's clearing. Eielson earned money delivering emergency shipments of goods and gathered popularity as an emergency air-ambulance flier. He was named "brother to the eagle" by local American Indians. With the figures from his summer's performance, Ben went "outside" that fall, back to Washington to bid for an Alaskan airmail contract.

With his Alaska congressional friend's aid, Eielson secured a ten-trip try-out airmail contract with a big, powerful biplane shipped to Fairbanks to be used to fly to the town of McGrath, a six-hundred-mile round-trip, once each two weeks, for which the post office would pay two dollars a flown mile. *But* the start-up was marked for February, when temperatures were far below zero. Ben nevertheless went up and succeeded, first using skis and, after the thaw, going back to wheels. He learned how to shield and warm the engine without setting it afire. Though Ben sometimes got lost for a while over the snowy wilderness, he never made a forced landing. No one before Ben had flown in Alaskan winter, which meant flying in the dark.

But returning from the eighth trip, the plane's wheels sank into muddy ground, and it went nose over. Damage was light, but when Eielson wired for parts, the post office replied by canceling the contract because it was impractical to fly aircraft in Alaska. Ben went back down to Washington. But even after long negotiations, he did not obtain another airmail contract; the dog-team interests underbid him. A contract to advise the army on ski planes expired, and a dispirited Eielson was back in the Dakotas trying to sell stocks and bonds when the call to join Wilkins came.

Working together at Fairbanks, Wilkins found himself to be comfortable with his pilot. Ben turned up the charm when necessary to the social situation, but otherwise his Norwegian background cut down small talk. Captain Wilkins, too, desired only essential conversation. In the meantime the expedition was making a jinxed start. One plane had burned at Detroit. The other two—new, unflown Fokkers—were enclosed-cabin high-wing monoplanes: the *Detroiter*, a big trimotor, and the *Alaskan*, a husky single-engine aircraft. Before either was flown, an expedition journalist strayed into a whirling propeller of the *Detroiter* and was killed.

On a day in early March 1926, the *Alaskan*, with Eielson piloting and Wilkins sitting at his side, took off on their maiden flight. Ben, who had never flown anything but open-cockpit biplanes, put the bigger cabin monoplane smoothly through the standard maneuvers until, on his landing approach, he came in high. Instead of going around to try again, as he'd likely do without his boss sitting close and evaluating, the pilot tried to correct the approach by slowing the Fokker. Wilkins has written that his fingers ached to seize the controls, but he refrained. The nose rose slightly as flying speed died away to the stall point. Like an elevator, the *Alaskan* dropped at least thirty feet, flat onto the end of the runway, and wrecked.

At least neither of the fliers was more than shaken up, and Wilkins gave out no opinion about the accident. They still had the bigger, better *Detroiter*, the tri-motor with the range to carry Wilkins all the way across to Spitsbergen. The next day Wilkins went up in the trimotor with the army's Major Lanphier piloting. Ghastly to relate, the *Detroiter* came in to land and it also came in high, similar pilot error that resulted in this plane also pancaking disastrously on nearly the same spot.

Again the aircrew were fortunate survivors, but the 1926 expedition had become a dodo. Rebuilding the planes would take a month for the *Alaskan*, six weeks for the *Detroiter*. By that time fogs rising from spring thaw would obliter-ate a search for new arctic islands. A telegram came from the frustrated stateside expedition backers demanding that both pilots be fired. Wilkins ignored it.

The captain then decided to use the rest of 1926's flying season to stockpile a base at Point Barrow, the northernmost Alaskan settlement, for 1927 explo-ration. No one had flown over this five hundred miles of lightly explored moun-tains and tundra until, on March 31, the repaired *Alaskan*, with Eielson piloting and Wilkins navigating, departed for Barrow.

In heavy clouds they flew toward the Endicott range, mapped with peaks as high as five thousand feet. Luckily the weather cleared and gave them a view of the real peaks, about twice as high as recorded. Beyond, a thick fog covered the tundra lands, a usual spring condition, as Wilkins knew. In his years with Stefansson, the Australian had often tramped the dreary Arctic Ocean coast near Point Barrow. So he didn't care about the soup, expecting they could descend over the ocean and buzz the shrouded coastline till Wilkins saw something he remembered, find Barrow, and land on the frozen beach.

Then, because they had been pushed by a strong tailwind and the fog ended at the ocean's edge, Wilkins abruptly decided to use the gasoline saved by the tail-wind's push, along with part of their cargo stock, and do some true exploring right away. Ben Eielson said it was okay with him. He had signed on to chauffeur this explorer wherever he wanted to go. Eielson's yen was not for adventure or scien-tific discoveries; rather, it was to gather and save money to enable him, if he sur-vived, to own an airline in Alaska.

Out beyond the Edge, penetrating a hundred miles into unexplored nowhere, the *Alaskan* droned above the eternal ice pack, climbing to nine thou-

THE TIRED *ALASKAN* EXPIRES. WHEN A WING FALLS OFF, THE PILOT IS LUCKY TO STILL BE ON THE GROUND. WILKINS IS IN THE FOREGROUND. *(Library of Congress)*

sand feet to get an overview far ahead. Wilkins was looking for new land and saw none. Returning to and finding Point Barrow was rather routine, and Wilkins silently rejoiced to know that his new pilot was fearless and reliable, a perfect companion for all the thrills and perils ahead.

The *Alaskan* continued to shuttle to Barrow, and crossing the high Endicotts always livened up the trip. Once, an unexpected lowering of cloud ceiling nearly finished them off after they had committed themselves to piercing a high pass. To be blinded in the woolly blankness was sure death, so they squeezed down dangerously low. Even the impassive Wilkins was stirred to warn of a rock wall closing in on the right, to which Ben's steady reply was, briefly, not to look at the really near one on the left. Deftly guided, the Fokker slipped through the bottleneck. Wilkins marveled to see their wheels turning because they had brushed against the snow. To Wilkins's thankful compliment Ben replied, "God held The Stick for me."[2]

Meanwhile the *Detroiter* had been rebuilt, and Wilkins wanted it on the Point Barrow shuttle. The big plane remained, however, at Fairbanks, because its army pilots feared to fly it over the high Endicott range, even though the *Detroiter* had three engines to the *Alaskan*'s one.

But then the *Alaskan's* propeller was disabled, and the replacement propeller did not function well. It caused two successive failures at takeoff from Fairbanks. Riding the bumpy ground beyond the runway caused structural damage to the plane, as Wilkins and Eielson learned on their next takeoff attempt—a wing fell off! Luckily they were still on the ground.

The next morning Wilkins herded the army pilots, Major Lanphier and Sergeant Wisely, aboard the loaded trimotor *Detroiter* and departed for Point Barrow. The plane flew well over the Endicotts and on above the usual pall of fog stretching toward Point Barrow. Captain Wilkins gave his pilots a Barrow compass bearing and retired to the back cabin to eat his lunch.

Sergeant Wisely was at the controls and very nervous about flying without sight of the ground, so he dove through the soup till he saw a north-flowing stream to follow. Captain Wilkins came forward and ordered a return to instrument navigation above the fog, and this was done. Wilkins returned to his lunch, but soon the aircraft began rocking and pitching. In the cockpit the two pilots were trying to fly in different directions! The nervous Wisely wanted to return to Fairbanks but was outranked and outwrestled by Major Lanphier, who took the *Detroiter* on into Point Barrow without further incident.

The persisting and expanding fogs of arctic summer soon ended the Point Barrow trips. Captain Wilkins did glimpse the passing *Norge* at Barrow. In a season of disappointments, that, at least, yielded him the secondary satisfaction of a scorned prophet proved right by others. Back in Detroit, Wilkins persuaded his backers to give him another opportunity at Alaskan polar flight in 1927.

In February, the Wilkins expedition gathered at Fairbanks. Except for Ben Eielson, there were mostly new faces. Pilot Alger Graham had been hired to fly support for the Wilkins-Eielson exploration flights. He came from Stinson Aircraft Company of Detroit, the makers and providers of two new enclosed-cabin biplanes. The Stinsons would be the aerial workhorses this season, though the trimotor *Detroiter* and twice-wrecked *Alaskan* were in reserve. At Point Barrow, Captain Wilkins was soon describing to Ben their first enterprise—to fly about 650 miles north into an ice-pack area marked "unknown" on the map and land there briefly for scientific purposes.

On March 29 Wilkins took advantage of a northward wind, circulating from an incoming coastal storm, to start the Stinson off with a strong tailwind. Far north of the Edge the weather turned fair and good for observation. At 550 miles out, however, their engine ran very rough, and a landing site was urgently sought.

Amundsen had claimed that no airplane on skis could survive an ice-pack landing, but Wilkins hurriedly selected a marginal area, where Eielson neatly landed the sputtering Stinson. Ben then worked on the engine alone, for science had priority with Wilkins. He eagerly carved two holes through the thick ice to enable an echo-sounding of ocean depth. When the first (correct) impulse registered a shocking three-mile depth, the scientist boldly asked the pilot to stop the engine so that the sounding could be carefully rechecked. Ben doubted the motor would restart, shrugged, and shut it off.

The pair did restart the Stinson, but its motor still ran roughly. When sunshine ceased, the fliers saw that their storm had turned and followed them. It took five attempts and much gasoline to get airborne; then within ten minutes the balky engine again made a landing necessary. Wilkins's arctic savvy picked out another ice haven, which they landed on safely. Both worked for a half hour overhauling the Stinson's ignition system amid flying snowflakes and were rewarded with a full roar from the 220-horsepower motor. In working bare-handed during the two stops in the minus thirty degrees chill, four fingers of Ben's right hand became critically frozen.

On a second attempt, they again escaped the ice pack, rising into a developing blizzard, their southward progress and their fuel being used up fighting a ferocious headwind. After a while they realized that they were not going to reach Point Barrow. At 9 P.M., in darkness and blizzard, the Stinson's engine stopped permanently and they began a blind, dead-stick descent from five thousand feet that neither expected to survive:

> Near the ground the air was rough. The plane swerved and pitched, but Eielson, still calm and cool, corrected with controls each unsteady move. In a moment we were in snowdrift. We could not see beyond the windows of the plane. I felt Ben brace himself against the empty gas tank; I leaned with my back against the partition wall of the cabin and waited; the left wing and skis struck simultaneously. We bounced and alighted as smoothly as if on the best prepared landing field. . . . Dimly about us I saw pressure ridges as high as the machine. . . .
>
> Ben looked at me and I looked at him. Then we began to laugh nervously and could not stop for about five minutes. Then Ben stretched out in a sleeping bag on top of the empty gas tank and I huddled in a corner of the cabin. We went to sleep.[3]

For five days blizzard and gale rocked the derelict Stinson, while beneath and around them the ice field shifted with wind stress, grating, groaning, shrieking, threatening to crush or split apart. The ice castaways wrote their story on the roof of the cabin, to which Wilkins carefully added the depth-sounding data. They subsisted on a plentiful supply of emergency rations and secured a bit of interior warmth by burning motor oil outside to heat objects and bringing them inside. Then came relative calm and the prospect of an eighty-mile-plus hike to the Alaska coast.

The expertise was shifted from Eielson's aerial skills to Wilkins's ice-pack savvy. Ben was only a tourist on the ice, but his captain's vast experience in arctic foot travel now was vital to their future. On the march, each dragged a sled cobbled together from aircraft scraps. Wilkins was prepared to live off animals met on the way if their high-energy food supply failed. Moreover, he was an expert navigator able to correct direction after each detour the ice-pack surface forced upon them.

Even on the level, the march was frustrating and exhausting. Snow cover hid sharp ice edges. Wilkins said that at times every fourth or fifth step ended in a tumble. Ice ridges were climbed achingly on hands and knees. Where young ice capped open water leads, they had to guess—then detour or slither carefully across. Wilkins built a snow house each night. He soon persuaded Ben to discard civilized clothing and live permanently in the smelly warmth of their Eskimo parka suits. One sleeping bag was kept to share for their feet.

Before a treacherous lead, Ben had his most heartsick moment. Just ahead, Wilkins plunged through the ice crust into seawater to his armpits, then heaved up mightily, and rolled quickly over the yielding ice to hardpan. Wilkins was soaked through and the temperature was far below zero. With haste the Australian shed his parka and footgear, ending by dancing naked on the ice pack! Ben feared him to be mad, but it was practical sanity. The subzero air was very dry, so Wilkins, prancing, briskly rubbed moisture from the parka suit onto snow powder. Then, reshod from supplies, with dry footgear, he put on the clammy parka again and miserably allowed body heat (over two days) to complete the drying.

Though extreme pain racked Eielson's frozen hand, he rarely mentioned it. As they trekked south the fingers blackened, and Wilkins feared that gangrene might develop. Finally on the eighteenth day, a higher ice ridge than any other came into view. The polar-wise explorer rejoiced, knowing it truly marked the Edge, pressing here against flat shore ice. Beyond that barrier, the pair exulted over the result of Wilkins's exact navigation, for in sight was the Eskimo village, Beechey Point, where they were able, for the first time in two weeks, to sleep in a wooden house.

Local opinion held that Eielson's frost-blackened fingers must be cut off immediately. Wilkins, agreeing, told Ben, who took the news "standing up," though the crude kitchen surgery "would mean the end of him as a pilot."[4] They were preparing to fill him with anesthetic whiskey and do the cutting, when, to the amazement of all, an airplane was heard at Beechey Point! It was Alger Graham, flying up from Fairbanks in the other Stinson, who had arrived solely because foul weather had denied him a Point Barrow landing.

Graham was in turn amazed to see his fellow fliers. He had flown air search missions in the early days but, like the others, had thought them to be frozen ice-pack corpses by now. Hustling Eielson aboard, he successfully flew into Barrow, where Ben received skilled attention from its physician, who amputated only two segments of the fifth finger and managed through lengthy treatment to save the rest of the pilot's guiding hand.

Graham's unexpected appearance and the isolated doctor's supreme skill were the last of the remarkable fortunate coincidences that allowed Wilkins and Eielson to be on hand to fly out of Alaska in 1928.

CHAPTER EIGHT

A STAR FLIES OUT OF ALASKA

THE DETROIT BACKERS OF WILKINS GAVE UP ON HIM after the 1927 season produced no spectacular polar records. Lindbergh had flown to Paris and was now a media star as "the Lone Eagle." That was the kind of aerial success story to sell to reimburse the cost of the venture. Airplane failures were common and their tales of little value. The Detroit backers held no ill will toward their arctic Australian—in fact they turned over to him the surviving aircraft—but the man just had no luck!

Wilkins, no quitter, now planned to become the lone eagle of the arctic. He decided to sell the *Detroiter* and *Alaska*. Then he'd go back to Point Barrow and, in the surviving Stinson biplane, fly northeast as far as it would go, alighting on the ice pack near a Canadian island or Greenland. En route he would settle the new-lands quest that had brought him and Stefansson far north fifteen years before. From the plane, he expected to trek to the nearest Eskimo outpost. Confidently self-sufficient on ice or land, he wouldn't care if it took a month or a year. Late in 1927, airplane salesman Wilkins was sitting in a San Francisco hotel room when the most attractive airplane he'd ever seen flew into view. The bright-orange-cabin monoplane's high wing was extraordinarily clean of strut and wire supports, and tight down on its streamlined fuselage. "It gave me the thrill that another might experience if he saw the ideal woman in the flesh."[1]

Captain Wilkins searched with fervor and eventually found the plane parked at the Oakland airport. The trim beauty was the first airplane designed and made at the new Lockheed Aircraft Company in Los Angeles. Designer Jack Northrop had named the model series Vega for one of the most luminous stars seen from Earth. The original Vega would soon fly in the Dole air race to Hawaii. This long-range capacity immediately connected in the explorer's brain: Why not get Ben Eielson as his pilot and navigate a Vega of his own all the way through from Barrow to Spitsbergen!

Wilkins eagerly went on down to Los Angeles where he found Allan Loughead, Lockheed's president, and Jack Northrop, the firm's head designer, willing to build a Vega modified for the explorer's special arctic needs. The Lockheed men became even more cooperative after Vega number one flew west in the Dole air race to Hawaii and vanished over the Pacific. That left them only Vega number two and the half-sold Vega number three project for Captain Wilkins.

The Australian's friendly advisers tried to dissuade him from his plan of buying an untried aircraft with a crash record of one for two. Eielson, who since his Alaskan ice-pack escape had been working for the government in certifying airplanes, was not enthusiastic about Vegas either, though he dutifully answered his captain's call and came west. Upon arrival, Ben witnessed a crash landing (another pilot-error stall on approach) of Vega number two. The pilot, a tester like Eielson for the government, bad-mouthed the Vega as being "hot," too fast for its controls. But Wilkins, who at this time had sold the trimotor Fokker to an aspiring Australian Pacific flier and the Stinson to plane-hungry Alaskan interests, as always went his own way and paid Lockheed to complete his dream Vega.

The bright orange and blue, clean-lined monoplane of spruce wood was powered by a Wright Whirlwind engine of 225 horsepower which could move the loaded aircraft along at up to 135 miles per hour. The prized unbraced wing, with a 41-foot span over a 27-foot fuselage, was only 18 inches thick but extra broad, with an area of 275 square feet. To manage a 2,700-mile nonstop range, bulky fuel tanks were added to the cabin to supplement the standard ones in the wing. Navigator Wilkins, separated from the pilot by the tanks (over which messages were passed), was aided by special side and bottom windows. Pilot and navigator had separate hatch entries.

Fortunately, Ben had a couple of weeks to practice flying Wilkins's Vega, named *Los Angeles*, before its shipment to Alaska. Ten to twenty landings per day comforted Eielson about handling this sleek monoplane. The flight north from Fairbanks

WILKINS STANDS IN THE REAR HATCH ENTRY. LATER HE WOULD HAVE A HARD TIME SQUIRMING INTO IT ON DEADMAN'S ISLAND. *(Lockheed Aircraft Company)*

passed favorably, so that around April 1 Wilkins and Eielson, without support personnel, were poised again at Point Barrow readying the ski-mounted Vega to fly out at the middle of the month when twenty-four-hour sunshine began on their route.

Wilkins rejected the easy navigational chore of going directly up to the Pole and down to Spitsbergen. To fly his desired course in the unknown area north of the Canadian islands, he figured to be making complicated course corrections every hour or so. Too, he could not rely on the standard compass because they would pass close to the magnetic pole situated within the nearby island archipelago. In that area good weather was needed both for celestial navigation and to search out possible new islands, but in their long journey toward Spitsbergen, they'd have to expect an encounter with foul weather. In a letter to his family, Ben matter-of-factly summarized the upcoming flight:

> In a few days we are going to cross the unexplored territory to the northeast. We hope to land at Kings Bay, Spitsbergen (2,200

miles away) but we may not be able to get any farther than Etah, Greenland (1,900 miles by the route we take) depending upon conditions. We have to take off with about 3,500 pounds of gasoline, etc. If we smash on the take-off, and there is always a good chance of it, I will not be able to get home till September—the first boat . . . [2]

Wilkins rounded up thirty Eskimos to shovel out a five-hundred-foot runway in the normal "airfield" area outside the village. He had to pay high wages—six dollars a day—to lure the men from their prejudice against doing menial work; in their society it was left for women. The overloaded Vega was not able to get off in that short distance and slammed past the runway's end, wrecking the metal skis. The reserve wooden set also failed, but wasn't destroyed.

A week's delay followed as dog teams pulled the Vega five miles to a new beach-lagoon takeoff area, where Wilkins ordered a one-mile runway shoveled and chipped out. The native crew took no interest in this further work. They

A DOG TEAM MOVES THE VEGA BETWEEN AIRSTRIPS. *(Smithsonian Air and Space Museum)*

already had the money they needed. Ben solved this problem by organizing rival Eskimo teams. Inspired to be best for the bragging competition at winter story times, the crews did finish the runway.

But it was only fourteen feet wide, and though the clean, high wing cleared the snow pile alongside, the lower planes of the Vega's tail, eleven feet five inches broad, did not. A swerve of only two feet while taking off was quite possible. . . .

On April 15, 1928, at about 10:00 A.M., the heavy orange-and-blue Vega slid away along the narrow runway gathering speed—the pilot reckoning they needed at least sixty miles per hour—as Wilkins was drawn to stare out a side window in tense fascination as the plane bumped and rocked on the slightly uneven surface. A sudden swing of that tail against the icy trench wall would end their expedition hopes and, perhaps, snuff out their lives. "Eielson kept his nerve. I prayed. Sixty, seventy miles an hour. We lifted, swung sickeningly, touched the ice again—then soared smoothly into free air."

In the cockpit, Ben, savoring their long-sought success, mockingly repeated the jibe printed in a Detroit newspaper, "If at first you don't succeed, Wilkins, *fly, fly, fly,* again!"[3]

The weather was fine, and Wilkins decided to fly low (500 to 800 feet) over the ice pack and study its varying patterns. A ground speed of 108 miles per hour was set to conserve fuel. At 500 miles out on the northeast course, ancient, heavy pack ice predominated, probably concentrated by pressure similar to the ice condition the *Norge* fliers noted around the "Ice Pole" at the center of the arctic pack. Islands were unlikely to be in that vicinity.

At 700 miles out the sky became overcast before them, obscuring the surface for a most frustrating 120 miles—a benign cloud mass they had to climb above to 3,000 feet. The few glimpses down through the pall showed the same old-ice patterns. Another shorter clear period ended with the Vega rising to 6,000 feet as it entered a region of great cumulus clouds rearing toward the stratosphere. Ben guided the plane along deep, meandering cloud corridors as his talented navigator passed a stream of correctional messages forward over the fuel tanks. Beginning in this area, the outside temperature of minus forty-eight degrees caused a roughening of the sound from the freezing Whirlwind engine. Eielson remedied this by spurts of accelerated climbs and descents, which heated the motor but boosted gasoline consumption from the plotted eleven to eighteen gallons per hour.

At about fourteen flying hours Wilkins reckoned they must be directly north of Grant Land (the north coast of Ellesmere Island) and was pleased to have the air navigation checked out. Amid towering cloud pillars, the coast's peaks glowed in the light of the midnight sun, a dancing red orb in the haze at the horizon toward the north. The exploration portion of the flight was over. Ahead, at north Greenland, Peary and others had mapped the landforms. In the line of flight from Point Barrow, the existence of half-believed Keenan Land, Crocker Land, and Harris Land were proven to be illusions, and Wilkins radioed back to Alaska "no foxes seen," as his code tip-off to certain scientists that there were no undiscovered islands remaining in the Canadian arctic.

After the Vega hummed through a stretch of heavy snowfall, the fliers again found a brief expanse of open visibility over north Greenland. It was mainly a view of a tremendous storm system lying to the south and east. Below was the first smooth ice pan they'd seen since Barrow capable of accepting the Vega without ruining its skis for a later takeoff. They'd been at it many hours and were fatigued, but, Wilkins thought, abnormally alert. "It was a hot, sandy, dried-up sensation. . . ."[4]

Ben, who had not had the navigator's opportunity to relieve his eyes by looking at the cabin interior, suffered from ice-pack glare "so bright it stabs the eye like a hot needle" and "the monotony of nothingness threatens to bludgeon one into insensibility . . ."[5]

It was stock-taking time, so the captain shoved a note ahead to his pilot:

> We are above the storm now; there are two courses open. Down there we can land and wait till it's over. Can we get off again? If we go on we will meet storm at Spitsbergen, and perhaps never find the land. Do you wish to land now?[6]

Wilkins said that his partner's head and shoulders wriggled as he thought it over. Relief would be great, but Ben also recalled that long, painful ice-field trek of just a year past. Sure, this storm might snow them in, and they'd have to hike out again. . . . Back over the tanks came Eielson's brief reply: "I am willing to go on and chance it."[7] Once again this pair thought alike.

As he had on their fateful flight onto the Alaskan ice pack, Wilkins used the approaching storm's outer circular wind movement to accelerate them around its northeast edge, then southwest, riding a current of cold air down to Spitsbergen at 120 miles per hour. But when the airstream they were riding collided with the warm air lurking over the Gulf Stream, they found themselves in turbulent storm conditions. Wilkins was sure they were over the Spitsbergen archipelago but dared not ask Ben to go down through the cloud cover, for fear of meeting a mountain head-on. Meanwhile the fuel gauge fluttered near zero.

Then a rift of cloud exposed two needle peaks and, beside them, a deep cloud crevice down to the sea. The fuel-light Vega spiraled into it, first bumping then bucking like a bronco. "Loose things in the cabin tumbled and rattled," recalled Wilkins. "With nothing to get a grip on I tumbled too if I didn't rattle."[8] Finally, there was ice-strewn water below, and so close was Eielson's final swoop that sea spray from furious storm winds drenched the cockpit windows then froze and obscured eighty percent of the pilot's forward vision.

As this occurred, both men glimpsed a flat snow pad flash by beneath them just before they faced a stern granite mountain and had to wheel the responsive Vega flat-out sideways, crabbing in the gale seaward before coming in again to seek a beach—but finding nothing but cliffs. The fuel level was critical. They needed to land and regroup for a fair-weather flight to search out King's Bay. So Wilkins resolved to find that flat island strip again. He still had good vision from his side windows, but communication must be written because Ben had become deaf from engine noise. So—glance and scribble madly, pass the note, look again and scribble!

> Turn right.
> Now to the left.
> A bit more.
> No, we have passed it.
> Turn back.
> Keep as close to the land as possible.
> There it is on the right.[9]

Finally the approach was lined up into the wind and, at the last moment, a fierce gust raised a pall of driven snow. Into the blinding whiteness dove steady-handed Ben, rewarded by the solid thump of skis and a smooth blind slide that ended *thirty feet ahead*, so strong was the headwind! Both fliers hurried out to drain the oil before it froze, to wrap the engine in its arctic muffler, and to stamp the snow flat and hard to freeze over the ski tops and prevent the wind from turning over the plane. Then, as on the Alaskan ice pack, they piled aboard and prepared to sleep. Twenty-and-a-half hours out of Alaska, twenty-five-hundred flown miles, their Lockheed Vega had carried them to safety beside Spitsbergen.

SNOW-MAROONED ON DEADMAN'S ISLAND. THIS IS A TIME-RELEASE EXPOSURE BY WILKINS. *(Library of Congress)*

For the next four days gales and intermittent snowfalls kept the pair sheltering in the Vega. Scouting the area in periods of good visibility revealed nothing but seascapes and mountains on a neighboring larger island and over on Spitsbergen proper a few miles to the east. The radio was useless because Wilkins had forgotten to reel in their trailing antenna during the hectic landing. Their island was too small to be on the flight map, but it was just as well they didn't know it was named Doedmansoeira—"Deadman's Island."

When the weather finally eased to a stiff breeze, they attacked the four-foot drifts, tramping and shoveling to make a one-hundred-foot downhill runway back out the ice pad they had landed on. Donning snowshoes, they stomped its surface smooth and hard. They had drained their gasoline and found twenty gallons, enough for their purpose once they got airborne. After the motor was heated by the stove carried for emergency starts, the Whirlwind awoke with a roar. Lightened by over a ton of expended fuel, Eielson expected to get off easily in the crosswind.

With both aboard and yearning to leave, the roaring Vega quivered but stayed stuck by frozen ski surfaces. Out leaped Wilkins to shovel them loose, but as the plane lurched ahead, he could not quite keep up. He missed his grasp for the hatch opening and fell back in the blown snow! The Vega got off. Fortunately Ben circled back, saw the frantically waving figure all alone on the snow, and landed again.

On the next try, the captain was again obliged to get out and push. This time a rope ladder hung over the side, secured to his entrance hatch. With the plane's forward movement, Wilkins tried to vault onto the fuselage ahead of the tail, squirm forward a bit, and grasp the rope ladder trailing in propeller blast. But his frost-stiffened fingers fumbled the webbing, and in desperation, he bit into the hemp with his teeth. A jerk from sliding sideways on the smooth fuselage surface convinced Wilkins that there was no future in dangling thus by his teeth beneath the soon-to-be-airborne Vega. So he let loose, was bopped by the tail, and fell dazed into a snowdrift at the runway's end.

Eielson landed again, and Wilkins shuffled up to the departure end, okay except for loosened front teeth. The landings had been hazardous in the crosswind and hard on the secondary skis. Also, the failed attempts had expended their slender fuel reserve. They resolved that if the next try failed, Wilkins would be left on his own with tent, food, and rifle. It was perilous to split up, but there was only this one last chance to fly to safe haven.

This time they raised the Vega's tail onto a block of packed snow, and Wilkins resorted to a new technique: They had a length of driftwood they'd brought up from the seaside. But it had proven too salt-soaked to burn. Now with one leg hooked inside the hatch and the other trying to brace against the fuselage side, the pusher used his heavy pole like a gondolier would and loosened the frost that immediately formed under the Vega's stationary skis.

Captain Wilkins strained mightily, and when the releasing jerk came, he was leaning far over and back. With extraordinary effort he arched back against the prop blast, as the engine raced, and tumbled helter-skelter into the cabin! The Vega climbed briskly to overlook the area. Immediately they spied a group of tall radio towers—the main Spitsbergen installation at Green Harbor—and within five minutes landed there.

As several station personnel skied down to greet them, their record flight was made official: 2,500 miles out of Point Barrow, Alaska; half or more over unexplored areas, navigating with precision across 171° of longitude without reliable magnetic compass readings; and carried with assurance all the way in the trim Lockheed Vega with its faithful Whirlwind engine.

They were acclaimed as the latest arctic heroes. The captain was dubbed Sir Hubert Wilkins by King George V of Great Britain, being honored not only for the recent triumph, but for twenty years of spectacular accomplishments in science and technology. American Carl Ben Eielson was awarded, among other medals, a rare peacetime Distinguished Flying Cross by the U.S. Army Air Service that had nurtured his flying career.

But before these honors were bestowed, within a month of the Wilkins-Eielson record-setting flight, the world's attention became riveted on a great and long-unfolding arctic air tragedy.

CHAPTER NINE

TRAGEDY OF THE *ITALIA*

WITHIN HOURS OF THE *NORGE'S* SAFE ARRIVAL IN ALASKA, the exultant Nobile was planning another polar airship flight from Europe, this one to be strictly Italian. In his factory he undertook designing a larger, specialized dirigible to fly over the Pole all the way to Tokyo! But in Italy other members in the Fascist government were jealous of his public acclaim. Nobile, it was said, had the knack of adding enemies like "honey attracts bees."[1] He was sidetracked from his polar project when sent to Japan as technical representative for the N-series dirigible that that nation had purchased.

By the time Nobile was able to return, his principal opponent, Italo Balbo, ruled Fascist aviation. Balbo believed long-range flying belonged to airplanes. He canceled the new polar dirigible project and ordered the destruction of what had already been built. In Italian aviation there was room at or near the top only for Italo Balbo.

But Nobile persisted, using his popular support. He talked to Mussolini, who eventually made a hard and safe bargain: General Nobile could take over the N-4, the last of the *Norge* series, if he could find private money to rent and insure it. The Italian Navy would supply flight officers and an expedition vessel, their cost also to be paid by Nobile and company. In this manner, if Nobile's expedition triumphed, the government would certainly take the credit; but if it failed—then it was Nobile's private disgrace. Mussolini was having it both ways at a profit.

The Italian Geographic Society sponsored General Nobile's polar expedition, and the city of Milan raised the money to pay for it. N-4, the *Italia*, was slightly modified, principally in having its hide toughened and slickened against hazards of propeller-driven ice bullets and ice deposits from the fog. Otherwise it was similar to the *Norge* in dimensions and operation. It was ready for the 1928 season.

Spitsbergen would be the *Italia*'s base. Flights were planned into unexplored areas north of Siberia, Greenland, and possibly Canada. Of course, the *Italia* would visit the North Pole again, and this time Nobile hoped to land personnel there for a limited time while the airship hovered above. The Pope gave General Nobile a cross that the expedition commander wanted to implant at the Pole. And if they had the luck to discover a previously unknown island, they'd have the means to descend and claim it for Italy! To

GENERAL UMBERTO NOBILE, AN AIR FORCE
GENERAL HOSTAGE IN A NAVY-CONTROLLED
OPERATION. *(Smithsonian Air and Space Museum)*

strengthen the flight's credentials in science, three distinguished professors of physics—Italian, Czech, and Swedish—would be aboard to perform varied tasks in monitoring the polar environment. And they wouldn't have Amundsen!

The *Italia* departed Milan on April 15, 1928, following a route around the eastern end of the high Alps, then north across central Europe to the German air station at Stolp, near the Baltic Sea. It was a shakedown voyage in the literal sense: The *Italia* was buffeted by a storm encountered early on, which put a fracture in its metal skeleton that reverberated through the bouncing aircraft. Next the dirigible survived an intense electrical storm, with lightning bolts darting near the very flammable hydrogen gas cells. So battered was *Italia* by the time it finished the twelve-hundred-mile course to Stolp that it was ten days before sufficient repairs were completed to allow proceeding on the next long hop of twenty-one hundred miles via Vadso, in north Norway, over the Barents Sea to King's Bay, Spitsbergen.

This journey was smoother, though *Italia*'s nose bashed into the mooring tower at Vadso, and one of the three 250-horsepower motors failed in the passage. At King's Bay, during maneuvering to get down and into the hangar, Nobile had his introductory clash with Captain Giuseppe Romagna Manoja of the expedition support vessel, *Citta di Milano*. Though its sailors assisted in guiding the airship to temporary berthing at Kings Bay's tower, they were abruptly withdrawn to their ship. In a wireless exchange with Nobile, Captain Romagna announced his independence, saying in substance: I take my orders from the navy at Rome, not from you, and dirigible handling is not a duty of ours. Nobile's own ground personnel had to rout out a force of Norwegian coal miners to walk *Italia* into shelter.

Nobile's first objective was to fly over the large, only partly observed Siberian arctic island of Severnaya Zemlya. The prospect of finding unknown territory seemed best in its vicinity. This ambitious plan failed on its first try because of foul weather and a frayed cable controlling the airship's rudder. Then it snowed heavily for two days at Kings Bay. Since the hangar was roofless, the *Italia* became dangerously weighted with sticking wet snow. A force of shovelers went

THE *CITTA DI MILANO* AT KING'S BAY, *ITALIA*'S DO-LITTLE EXPEDITION HEADQUARTERS.
(Library of Congress)

THE *ITALIA*, READY TO DEPART KING'S BAY. *(Library of Congress)*

aloft, trampling and shoveling furiously on the dirigible's topside. After the crisis eased, repairs were made on tears in *Italia*'s outer covering caused by shovel tips and hobnailed boots.

On May 15 Nobile again steered the *Italia* toward Severnaya Zemlya, 1,000 miles to the northeast. The weather varied markedly during the 69-hour flight, and a strengthening sidewind blowing from the north at more than 25 miles per hour finally denied the expedition a survey of their objective. *Italia*'s three engines, totaling 750 horsepower, did not cope well with driving the bulky dirigible in heavy winds, even though they used large amounts of fuel. On this historic, looping journey the *Italia* flew 2,400 miles and explored 17,250 square miles of unknown, empty ice pack. It also recorded much finer details about known arctic territories.

After a few days' rest for the aircrew, and a gas leak repair on the dirigible, the Nobile expedition departed for the North Pole on May 23. Sixteen, plus one (Titina, of course) were aboard the *Italia*. Most of the blue-collar aircrew had flown with the *Norge*. So had Finn Malmgren, the Swedish meteorologist. Newcomers

PROFESSOR MALMGREN, THE DESPON-
DENT FORECASTER. *(Library of Congress)*

included four officers of the Italian Navy, two scientists, the journalist from Mussolini's newspaper, and the radio man (wireless operator). The only person with any experience on the arctic surface was their Swedish weatherman.

The atmosphere, sparklingly clear over Spitsbergen, darkened into fog below them after they crossed the edge of the ice pack. Their route carried them to Greenland's northeast corner, then into the unexplored lane between Peary's passage on land and the area where the *Norge* had flown. As the weather lightened, a tremendous tailwind developed. The airship zipped along at 62 miles per hour. Their altitude of 750 feet allowed a lookout of 60 miles to either side—but there was no land, only monotonous ice glare. The North Pole, though, was shrouded by an impressive castle of clouds. Dismissing the landing scheme, the flags and the Pope's cross were thrown down from 450 feet. Seven of the men and one dog shared the unique experience of having been over the North Pole twice.

Nobile consulted meteorologist Malmgren. Would the stiff wind persist? If so, he thought that rather than buffet the *Italia* against such a tough headwind, he'd let the airship ride the tailwind down to Canada. The Swede weatherman objected with two points: Returning to King's Bay would help the studies of the scientists aboard, and it was much closer. He also felt, after reading weather reports, that there would be an early end to the south wind that was impeding their progress. Indeed, it might well turn about and push them home, as well. Nobile decided to return to Spitsbergen.

But the contrary wind persisted and butted the airship's bulk from the southwest. The repeated advice of Malmgren was to push on as fast as possible to emerge from the area of the headwind. The three engines strained, and air speed was sixty miles per hour, but ground speed was below thirty miles per hour. Fuel was being used at an alarming rate. The headwind not only slowed the *Italia*, it also bucked and bounced it, driving the dirigible off course to the eastward. This went on for thirty hours as the mood aboard grew quiet and grim.

Cloud layer above, fog below—the aircrew scarcely knew where they were. Their twice-hourly wireless contact with Captain Romagna's *Citta di Milano* gave them a directional heading only. At one point Nobile guided the *Italia* westward in rough compensation for the wind. But he didn't persevere because the wind then drove them sideways northward. To get data on drift, the navigators had to see the pack below, and lowering the *Italia* into the mists added ice to the aircraft's outer covering. Soon the gunshotlike noise of propeller-launched ice chunks breaking holes in the undercarriage reverbrated as it had on the *Norge*.

At 9:25 A.M. on May 25, the helmsman suddenly cried out that the elevator control had jammed with the nose down, and the altitude was only 750 feet. The commander ordered all engines stopped. The fuel-light dirigible equalized at 250 feet and began to rise. As they ascended, a crew member risked a sharp rap to the control lever with the heel of his hand, and elevator control returned to normal. Since the sky was lightening, they decided to get a sun shot. As they cleared the clouds at 2,700 feet, all looked south yearning to see peaks—there were none. At 3,300 feet, pressure in the rear cells was too high, and Nobile valved off some hydrogen.

The navigators decided they were 180 miles northeast of King's Bay (quite close, however, to the uninhabited eastern portion of the huge Spitsbergen archipelago). During the next wireless transmission, Nobile failed to report the newly determined position. Also, radio operator Giuseppe Biagi, frightened by the elevator problem, gossiped to his buddy on the *Citta di Milano*: ". . . you are lucky . . . if I am late answering there is a reason. . . ."[2]

The *Italia* descended to regain visual contact with the surface. Then at 10:30 A.M. a shout of grave alarm came from the helmsman. "We are heavy!"[3] The airship was sagging at the rear, then falling from about eight hundred feet. Nobile immediately ordered a full surge of propeller power, but there was no effect. Their fall accelerated past two feet per second as the commander sent a rigger to find out what was deflating buoyancy in the stern gas cells. But there was no time—the ice field seemed to rush up, ugly and knobby. Ignition switches were turned off on all engines just before the rear pod struck the ice pack.

In reaction the dirigible tilted forward, slamming the command cabin onto the pack, where it disintegrated as it was crushed into the snow and ice and spewed out equipment and men. Two or three survivors came to their senses immediately. Peering up into the torn bulk of the gasbag hovering near, they saw Ettore Arduino, the engine chief, standing on the keel-girder passageway alertly pitching down emergency supplies stored in the vicinity, including a tent. He likely expected the collapse of the gas cells, but this did not occur. In a moment the implacable wind lifted the lightened gasbag, and Arduino and five others in the upper section were carried up and away into the arctic mist aboard the hopelessly derelict *Italia*.

General Nobile lay with a broken arm and leg and painful contusions, expecting to die. Natale Cecioni, the *Italia*'s chief mechanic, suffered an ugly compound leg fracture. Failed weather forecaster Malmgren had a dislocated shoulder; he talked of suicide in the early days of ice exile, but was dissuaded. Naval officer Filippo Zappi had bruised ribs; his colleagues Adalberto Mariano, Felice Trojani, and Alfredo Viglieri were okay, as was radioman Biagi. Czech Professor Frantisek Behounek, oldest of the party, was in fair condition. And Titina frisked amid the wreckage unconcerned. The motorman of the rear pod, Vincenzo Pomella, a *Norge* veteran, had been killed on impact.

As the ice castaways recovered from shock, they found a great amount of vital supplies strewn about, eventually enough to support the party for about forty-five days. Nobile realized he wasn't expiring, and Biagi recalled that, at the last moment, he had seized the emergency wireless set (his footstool) and clutched it to his chest. Biagi now searched in the snow nearby and found it. Shaking the box, he heard no rattle or tinkle of broken tubes—just the gurgle of the brandy bottle hidden inside, also intact. So he set about erecting an aerial shaped from flotsam tubing wrenched out of the airship. A half hour after the crash, Biagi spotted a pillar of smoke ten to fifteen miles northeast, the fiery end of the *Italia*.

With the tent came a sleeping bag, which they cut to hold both fracture cases (and Titina). They took up half the tent meant for four. Six others (one man always on lookout) slept layered. Nobile remarked that all of this togetherness did much to warm the interior. The tent was streaked and tinted red with salvaged dye markers. They were less than fifty miles from eastern Spitsbergen, coping and initially hopeful that the radio signal Biagi faithfully tapped out at the agreed hours would stir a reply from, and action on, the *Citta di Milano*.

But days, then a week, passed without result. Biagi listened to a Europe guessing their fate and talking vaguely of searching for them in the wrong places. The *Citta di Milano* radio was very active with the speculations of the reporters as well as ordinary radio traffic. It was as if, as far as their expedition

IN THE FORTY-EIGHT-DAY CAMP ON THE ICE PACK, FROM LEFT: BEHOUNEK, BIAGI, CECIONI (SEATED), VIGLIERI, AND (CENTER) THE "WORLD'S MOST IMPORTANT RADIO STATION." *(Library of Congress)*

headquarters were concerned, the *Italia* survivors didn't exist! It is hard to imagine the frustration there on the ice. Malmgren predicted gloomily that the current would carry them northeast. Zappi and Mariano began agitating for most of the able-bodied men to march south to visible coastal islands.

Meanwhile, the *Citta di Milano* was completely useless because of the stupidity and ambivalence of Captain Romagna. When a few periods for good reception had passed in silence, Romagna concluded that the *Italia* had crashed and Nobile and crew were likely dead, or at least unable to signal. So he instructed his radio staff not to bother listening anymore! They busied themselves instead with the increased radio traffic the mystery generated. And as a self-protecting, time-serving officer, he eluded further action by referring the affair to Rome.

The expedition wasn't an official one of the government, so the bureaucrats passed the problem around. Finally, it was left up to aviation minister Italo Balbo, a nonsupporter of Nobile's project. He had turned down the explorer's request for search-and-rescue planes to be stationed in Spitsbergen. Now he informed grieving crew relatives that no planes could be dispatched until the *Italia* was found.

Italo Balbo had heard that the *Italia* was not insured; if that were so, General Nobile was in big trouble!

Out on the ice pack, all the navy officers argued about leaving for barren islands seen in the distance. No one but Nobile and Biagi thought the radio was working properly. The expedition commander insisted that adequate staff remain to care for those who could not travel. Finally, Zappi and Mariano talked arctic expert Malmgren into going, and the trio prepared to leave. Fortunately, Malmgren was able to bravely creep near a negligent polar bear and shoot it with a salvaged handgun—450 pounds of meat!

The coast-seeking party departed at the beginning of June, making very slow progress. From camp they were still visible in the distance more than a day later. Nobile had Biagi step up his transmission length to an hour at a time, despite the battery drain. This transmission was received on the evening of June 3 by a Russian amateur radio operator living near the White Sea port of Archangel, well over a thousand miles away. He reported it, and in Rome they knew of the *Italia* survivors' SOS on June 6, which Biagi heard from a Rome broadcast. On the evening of June 8, the *Citta di Milano* finally sought radio contact. It had taken two weeks to establish communications, which prudent conduct aboard the expedition vessel should have achieved right away.

Meanwhile, even before the contact, formal search-and-rescue operations from the air forces of Norway, Sweden, and Finland had started. The Scandinavian nations committed handfuls of planes and support vessels. Russia dispatched two icebreakers that carried scout aircraft. Shamed by a bad press and foreign officials' pressure, Italy finally dispatched a pair of first-class flying boats to King's Bay. Nobile's adversary, Amundsen, enthusiastically volunteered to search for the lost Italians, and a French aviator flew in his flying boat to pick up Amundsen and his colleague Dietrichson. Britain and the United States, nations owning long-range dirigibles, declined to participate for technical reasons.

This gathering and preparation to the south took many days, while shifting winds moved the ice pack hither and yon. Nobile says that the stupidity in the wireless room of the *Citta di Milano* did not end when contact was renewed. The expedition ship often transmitted to them but would quickly sign off without listening to Nobile's position corrections. Life on the pack ground on—they had dreary food and shelter, which once had to be painfully moved to a safer ice floe. Bears came three times; two had fled amid ineffectual shots from the handgun Malmgren had kindly left, and one was sped on its way by the little dog, Titina.

THE RED TENT, AS SEEN FROM MAJOR MADDALENA'S FLYING BOAT ON JUNE 20, 1928. *(Library of Congress)*

On June 17 the castaways' spirits were strengthened as they saw two airplanes led by Riiser-Larsen of the Norwegian group circling to the south of them. In following days aircraft were seen closer, but the airmen were unable to pick out the tiny red tent in the shimmering vastness of the ice desert. On June 18 the Amundsen party of six, piloted by René Guilbaud, departed from Tromsö, in northern Norway. Flying toward King's Bay, they vanished. Thereafter the air searchers sought three parties: Nobile, Malmgren, and Amundsen.

It was a big, radio-equipped Italian flying boat, piloted by Umberto Maddalena, that spotted the red tent on June 20 and dropped supplies. Both Italian planes came late on June 21st and parachuted many more relief goods. On a final pass, Pier Penzo's plane nearly scraped the tent top as those aboard heartily yelled down "*Arrivederci!*"[4] The greasy, fishy bear-meat diet was now varied by baked and canned foodstuffs, and they obtained medicines, new footgear, rubber boats.

Next came the turn of the Swedish Air Force, which established a temporary base on the shore ice at Northeast Land, Spitsbergen. Their fliers located Nobile's camp and along with supplies dropped a note asking that a landing area be scouted, for they had one Fokker biplane with skis. This was done to their satisfaction, and on the day-night of June 23, Nobile saw a seaplane and the ski-mounted Fokker approaching. Joy and suspense beat in the hearts of the men as the ski plane made two light exploratory drags across the landing area and settled on the third pass, halting fifteen yards short of an ugly ice obstruction.

Pilot Einar Lundborg stepped down as copilot Birger Schyberg kept the engine carefully running. Viglieri and Biagi escorted him to the tent where Cecioni, with the compound fracture, was waiting to travel. Lieutenant Lundborg made it politely clear to Nobile that his orders were to carry out the *Italia* commander on the first trip. Thereafter he would shuttle the others out one at a time. Though Nobile assumed the "order" came from Rome, it was the naive brainchild of Captain Egmont Tornberg, commanding the Swedes. Unaware of Italian political intrigues, he sought to displace the hesitating Captain Romagna as search coordinator by bringing activist General Nobile to King's Bay.

The expedition commander reacted heatedly: It must be poor Cecioni first; then Trojani, ill with stomach pains; and Professor Behounek . . . But Lundborg was implacable; he'd come for Nobile. Anyway, Cecioni was a large man, too heavy for the little Fokker carrying Schyberg, too. He promised to come back right away, alone, and take out Cecioni. So aided by the urging of the others, Nobile agreed to go out first to get to work on shaping up the *Citta di Milano*. Not slow on the uptake, Titina romped ahead, made friends with Schyberg, and was already snuggled in the Fokker when they boarded.

Nobile was flown to the Swedish encampment. Lundborg honored his promise to return alone (with a wingman). But the Fokker's engine ran roughly, and he turned aside to land near a coastal island. When the disturbance cleared—probably a bit of water in the fuel—the brave Swede continued his mission, and about 3 A.M. the watchers on the floe saw him landing. At a precarious moment, the engine again roughened and weakened. The little biplane hit the surface instead of touching it; a ski tip dug under, and over the plane went, propeller and skis smashed. Mopping a bloodied nose, the cursing Lundborg plainly saw that he had permanently exchanged himself for Nobile! Cecioni wept in frustration.

When General Nobile had been transferred to the *Citta di Milano*, Captain Romagna looked at him critically and said, "People might criticize you for coming first, General. It would be well to give some explanations."[5] Nobile retorted that he had been ordered out, but Romagna truly knew nothing of that. The declaration by Nobile to Rome that "I have come to take up my post of command" was rejected, and Captain Romagna was pointedly left in charge.[6] Wild stories

SAFELY OUT AT THE SWEDE'S CAMP, NOBILE FEEDS TITINA. *(Library of Congress)*

appeared in the world's newspapers: Nobile had rushed to planeside (on a broken leg!), elbowed others aside in his frantic haste to be first out. Such mudslinging suited Nobile's political enemies.

Daily prodding Romagna, Nobile was sometimes able to accomplish a little. The captain took orders from Rome, though, and Rome told him to go slow—don't risk personnel, et cetera. A German offer to send up a Dornier Wal was turned down. Romagna reported the area was too congested! Though the Italian fliers found technical reasons not to go over the Red Tent, the Swedes continued and sent back to secure another ski plane. The Italians convinced the Finns not to risk their larger ski-equipped airplane in the substandard ice-field landing strip. The Norwegians were preoccupied searching for Amundsen. Meanwhile, the Malmgren party was long overdue on the coastal islands.

So it was a good thing that the Russians were coming! On July 1 the icebreaker *Krassin* passed Cape North nearing the target area off Northeast Land. But the ice pack was sometimes six feet thick. The icebreaker's method was to ram against the solid ice with its armored prow running up topside and the vessel's weight crunching down and through. In the midst of these efforts, the *Krassin's* left propeller was broken. They might have given up then, except for an

THE ICE PRISONERS USE LUNDBORG'S TIPPED FOKKER. NOTE THE RUBBER BOAT IN FRONT. (*Library of Congress*)

impassioned appeal direct from the *Italia's* commander that they continue, which they did. So the hospitalized Nobile was able to take a hand in the rescue breakthrough, physical and moral.

On July 6 the Swedes landed another small ski-equipped plane on the melting, deteriorating strip beside the famed Red Tent, now moved to use the tipped Fokker as living annex. Lieutenant Schyberg had a written order to the castaways' commander, Viglieri, that he was to bring out the Swede's own Captain (promoted on the ice pack) Lundborg. He'd loathed the two weeks he'd been an ice prisoner. His companions had served six weeks and didn't place much stock in the pilots' claim that they'd be back for them. If there was hope, it was now set on the *Krassin*.

Krassin carried a good-sized scout plane, a Junkers, that operated from level ice fields beside the vessel. On July 10, during a bright spot in a foggy spell, the fliers risked another search mission. Suddenly the ship heard brief, stirring news: "Malmgren group." Contact then ceased; weather worsened. Hours later the tension aboard the fog-wrapped *Krassin* was ended. The plane radioed that they had safely crash-landed at an island, and pilot Boris Chukhnovsky urged: "Having food for two weeks, consider it imperative that *Krassin* go to Malmgren's aid soonest, without worrying about us. . . ."[7] then gave navigation coordinates to reach at least two men huddled on a small ice floe in a meltwater lake.

It took a day and a half for *Krassin* to crush through and pick up the two men from their miserable perch in a fast-decaying ice field. They were the Italian naval officers Zappi, alert and better clothed than Mariano, emaciated, frozen, nearly dead. Where was Malmgren? Zappi pointed under the ice. His health had broken and, on June 14, the older Swede had asked to be left to his fate. They unwillingly agreed and had camped within sight for a day to allow him to reconsider. But from a distance Malmgren weakly waved them off and lay down; and so they had traveled on . . . vainly till today's miracle. Ugly, unsubstantiated rumors of cannibalism arose after the officers' recitations.

Twelve hours later, as guided by radio corrections and finally a smoke pillar glimpsed between banks of fog, the *Krassin* reached the men at the Red Tent at 9:35 P.M., on July 12. Viglieri, Behounek, Biagi, crippled Cecioni, and Trojani had been on the ice pack forty-eight days! And without the *Krassin* they would soon have been at sea in rubber boats—"our navy," Biagi called them—for high summer was fast thawing the edge of the solid ice. And so the surviving *Italia* crew was ferried to reunion with General Nobile and political muzzling by Captain Romagna. In closing this episode, it must be noted that the *Krassin* was the personal inspiration of professor Rudolf Samoilovitch, a geologist from Leningrad, who got the permission, crewed the previously idle vessel, and directed its successful mission from aboard.

THE RUSSIAN ICEBREAKER *KRASSIN* IN THE ICE PACK WITH ITS SCOUT AIRPLANE. *(Library of Congress)*

Over Nobile's strenuous objection, an extended search to discover the airship's fate was thought too dangerous and futile. Considering the implacable arctic wilderness and the primitive aircraft of the 1920s, it was a remarkable sequence of good fortune that more of the rescuers did not come into harm's way. Major Penzo, flying one of the Italian flying boats south, crashed in France, killing himself and two others; and then there were the six of Amundsen's party.

The Norwegian search for the fate of a national hero was thorough. Probably, as radio contact ceased after two and a half hours, Amundsen's group didn't cross the water, but instead had a violent collision with it, or broke up afterward on its rough surface. A few bits of identifiable wreckage were eventually retrieved. Though Amundsen did not die in true arctic circumstances as he might have wished, losing his life while going to the aid of a fellow explorer was no ill way for him to end.

WHATEVER HAPPENED TO...?

THERE WAS LITTLE HIGH-ARCTIC FLYING FOLLOWING THE *Italia* disaster, so we can consider the era of rough-and-ready pioneer arctic flying over by 1928. When in 1937 the Russians established near the Pole a temporary (nine months) weather station, supplied by plane, and made two record-setting transpolar flights to the United States, it was with a decade's improvement in equipment and aerial technology. The breaching of the arctic's remoteness by technology continues into the present.

In 1958 the nuclear submarine USS *Nautilus* crossed under the ice pack end to end, from Alaska to the east side of Greenland, by way of the North Pole; in 1968 Ralph Plaisted, of Minnesota, and three others drove snowmobiles to the Pole along Peary's route; in 1977 a nuclear-powered Soviet icebreaker, *Arktika*, lunged through the ice to the Pole from Siberia; and the next year, Japanese adventurer Naomi Uemura drove a dogsled team by himself on Peary's track, but he was resupplied by air and flew back after reaching the North Pole.

Air passengers now cross over the Edge from side to side on various polar routes, pioneered by SAS (Scandinavian Airlines System) in 1954. Daily, planeloads of business travelers, tourists, grandmothers, and infants ride in climate-controlled comfort seven miles above the eternal ice pack on routes between Europe and the Orient. In this jet age General Nobile could have realized his dream of 1926 to make a nonstop transpolar flight from northern Europe to Tokyo. It happens every day in about eleven flying hours.

But back in Italy, his enemies saw to it that Nobile was tried and disgraced officially. General Nobile emigrated to the Soviet Union, establishing a dirigible program there in the 1930s. Toward the end of that decade, his teenage daughter pressured the widower to quit the Russia of Stalin's purges, and they returned to obscurity in Italy. His offer to serve during World War II was scorned, but in the new postwar democratic era he became officially rehabilitated. The longest-living veteran of polar air pioneering (ninety-three), Nobile was able to repair his popular reputation later in interviews with writers still interested in the *Italia* tragedy.

Let's briefly look into the fortunes of other polar fliers:

Walter Wellman lived on into the 1930s, apparently remote from aeronautics. Of the six fliers who went down with the Dornier Wals onto the ice pack in 1925, Amundsen and Dietrichson crashed and died together, soon followed by Omdal who vanished in a transatlantic flight attempt. Riiser-Larsen survived, however, to eventually head up the Norwegian Air Force, and died in bed after a well-fulfilled career. The German mechanic Feucht emigrated to Argentina. Ellsworth's exploration career continued in high gear until he was disabled by a fall in the Grand Canyon in the early 1940s.

Ellsworth, Byrd, and Wilkins were all drawn to the last frontier of antarctic exploration. Though Wilkins and Eielson were the first to fly down there, it was Byrd who, in 1929, added a flight over the South Pole to match his now-soiled North Pole claim. He became America's most popular explorer during his Antarctic period—particularly while broadcasting from "Little America," where he stayed alone for several months. But, his popular activities isolated Admiral Byrd from the mainstream U.S. Navy, which did not assign him a first-line command in World War II.

After an antarctic season flying with Wilkins, Ben Eielson hurried north with the money to achieve his dream of owning and operating an Alaskan airline. Sadly, it was only months later that he was killed in a Bering Sea-area crash during a flight to pick up a cargo of furs. Flight conditions were poor; he was foolish to go. It was rumored that Eielson was responding to a spurious dare from a competitor. Ben is remembered in Alaska by mighty Mount Eielson, and also by Fairbanks's Eielson Air Force Base.

It should not be a surprise that Sir Hubert Wilkins thought of a project to travel *under* the Edge to the North Pole. He was supported by Lincoln Ellsworth in the 1931 experiments. The American surplus submarine he named *Nautilus* was too worn out to do more than prospect under the fringe of the ice pack, but it was still a notable first.

By then Sir Hubert was happily married to an Australian actress he had met in America. In later years he worked steadily doing arctic research for the U.S. Armed Forces till his death, at 70, in 1958, the same year the U.S. Navy's nuclear *Nautilus* cruised under the North Pole. By the arrangement of his widow, Wilkins's ashes were carried aboard the USS *Skate*, which in 1959 surfaced right at the North Pole, its conning tower thrusting up through the ice pack. They opened the hatch into a typical arctic blizzard and scattered Sir Hubert's ashes to the winds. . . .

What a way for a flying polar hero to go!

ENDNOTES

EPIGRAPH (p. ix)

Andrée, quoted in *Challenge to the Poles*, John Grierson, 1961.

CHAPTER ONE

1. "The Fate of Andrée," *Geographical Journal*, November 1930.

2. "The Andrée Tragedy," Naboth Hedin. *American-Scandinavian Review*, November 1930.

3. "A Swedish Film Recreates a Daring Flight That Failed," R. T. Kahn. *Smithsonian*, May 1983.

4. "Andrée's Flight Into the Unknown," Jonas S. Stadling. *Century Magazine*, November 1897.

5. Quoted in *Wings of Mystery*, Dale Titler, 1966.

6. From Andrée's diary, as quoted in *Challenge to the Poles*, John Grierson, 1961.

CHAPTER TWO

1. *The Aerial Age*, Walter Wellman, 1911.

2. *The Aerial Age*, Walter Wellman, 1911.

3. *The Aerial Age*, Walter Wellman, 1911.

4. *The Aerial Age*, Walter Wellman, 1911.

CHAPTER THREE

1. *My Life as an Explorer*, Roald Amundsen, 1927.

2. *My Life as an Explorer*, Roald Amundsen, 1927.

3. *My Life as an Explorer*, Roald Amundsen, 1927.

4. *My Life as an Explorer*, Roald Amundsen, 1927.

5. *My Life as an Explorer*, Roald Amundsen, 1927.

6. *Beyond Horizons*, Lincoln Ellsworth, 1938.

7. *Beyond Horizons*, Lincoln Ellsworth, 1938.

CHAPTER FOUR

1. *Beyond Horizons*, Lincoln Ellsworth, 1938.

2. *My Polar Flight*, Roald Amundsen, 1925.

3. Quoted in *Challenge to the Poles*, John Grierson, 1961.

4. Quoted in *Two Against the Ice*, Theodore Mason, 1982.

5. *Beyond Horizons*, Lincoln Ellsworth, 1938.

6. *My Polar Flight*, Roald Amundsen, 1925.

7. *Beyond Horizons*, Lincoln Ellsworth, 1938.

8. *Beyond Horizons*, Lincoln Ellsworth, 1938.

9. *Challenge to the Poles*, John Grierson, 1961.

CHAPTER FIVE

1. Quoted in *Struggle*, Charles J. V. Murphy, 1928.

2. *Skyward*, Richard E. Byrd, 1928.

3. Quoted in *Struggle*, Charles J. V. Murphy, 1928.

4. Quoted in *Struggle*, Charles J. V. Murphy, 1928.

5. *My Life As an Explorer*, Roald Amundsen, 1927.

6. *Beyond Horizons*, Lincoln Ellsworth, 1938.

7. *Beyond Horizons*, Lincoln Ellsworth, 1938.

8. *Skyward*, Richard E. Byrd, 1928.

9. *Skyward*, Richard E. Byrd, 1928.

CHAPTER SIX

1. *Beyond Horizons*, Lincoln Ellsworth, 1938.

2. *First Flight Across the Polar Sea*, Roald Amundsen, 1926.

3. Quoted in *Ships in the Sky*, John Toland, 1957.

4. *Beyond Horizons*, Lincoln Ellsworth, 1938.

5. *At the North Pole*, Lincoln Ellsworth, 1927.

CHAPTER SEVEN

1. Quoted in *Brother to the Eagle*, Erling Rolfsrud, 1952.

2. Quoted in *Brother to the Eagle*, Erling Rolfsrud, 1952.

3. Quoted in "Over the Top of the World," Vilhjalmur Stefansson. *American Magazine*, September 1928.

4. *Sir Hubert Wilkins*, Lowell Thomas, 1961.

CHAPTER EIGHT

1. *Flying the Arctic*, George H. Wilkins, 1928.

2. Quoted in *Brother to the Eagle*, Erling Rolfsrud, 1952.

3. *Flying the Arctic*, George H. Wilkins, 1928.

4. *Flying the Arctic*, George H. Wilkins, 1928.

5. Quoted in *Brother to the Eagle*, Erling Rolfsrud, 1952.

6. Quoted in *Challenge to the Poles*, John Grierson, 1961.

7. Quoted in *Challenge to the Poles*, John Grierson, 1961.

8. *Flying the Arctic*, George H. Wilkins, 1928.

9. Quoted in *Challenge to the Poles*, John Grierson, 1961.

CHAPTER NINE

1. Quoted in *Target: Arctic*, George Simmons, 1965.

2. Quoted in *Target: Arctic*, George Simmons, 1965.

3. *My Polar Flights*, Umberto Nobile, 1961.

4. *My Polar Flights*, Umberto Nobile, 1961.

5. *My Polar Flights*, Umberto Nobile, 1961.

6. *My Polar Flights*, Umberto Nobile, 1961.

7. Quoted in *Target: Arctic*, George Simmons, 1965.

BIBLIOGRAPHY

A Selection of Further Reading

There are two excellent histories that carry the record of arctic (and antarctic) flight from the last century up to the 1960s:

Challenge to the Poles, John Grierson. Hamden, CT: Archon Books, 1964.
Target: Arctic, George Simmons. Philadelphia, PA: Chilton Books, 1965.

Less polar coverage, but a fine book is:

Oceans, Poles, and Airmen, Richard Montague. Random House, New York 1971.

Most of the pioneer polar airmen wrote books about their accomplishments, which are the prime, fascinating sources for *Over the Edge*. Because they were written long ago and most have not been reprinted, these books will most likely be found in larger, long-established libraries. A list of books follow, arranged in the order of the chapters of this book:

Andrée's Story, Salomon Andrée. 1930. Reprint, New York: Viking, 1960. Includes the diaries discovered with the dead men's bodies on White Island.

Unsolved Mysteries of the Arctic, Vilhjalmur Stefansson. 1938. New York: Books for Libraries Press, 1972. The veteran arctic explorer's chapter on Andrée is fine commentary.

The Aerial Age, Walter Wellman. New York: A. R. Keller, 1911. His autobiography of flight, without much bragging or evasion.

The Motor Balloon America, Edward Mabley. Brattleboro, VT: Stephen Greene Press, 1969. A 94-page biography of Wellman's airborne career.

My Life as an Explorer, Roald Amundsen. Garden City, NY: Doubleday, Page, 1927. Amundsen's story, ending with his vendetta with Nobile.

Beyond Horizons, Lincoln Ellsworth. Garden City, NY: Doubleday, Doran, 1938. Growing up rich but unfulfilled—until Amundsen. Those adventures plus Antarctica.

Our Polar Flight, Roald Amundsen and Friends. New York: Dodd, Mead, 1925. First-person accounts of the ice pack adventure aboard N24 and N25.

First Crossing of the Polar Sea, Roald Amundsen and Lincoln Ellsworth. New York : George S. Doran, 1927. Triumphal flight of the *Norge* detailed.

Skyward, Richard E. Byrd. 1928. Chicago: Lakeside Press, 1981. Well-crafted autobiography from childhood to North Pole trip.

The Last Explorer, Edwin P. Hoyt. New York: John Day, 1968. The complete Byrd, including Antarctica.

Floyd Bennett, Cora Bennett. New York: W. F. Payson, 1932. He died too young. His wife's perky biography of Byrd's indispensable associate.

Flying the Arctic, George H. Wilkins. New York: G. P. Putnam's Sons, 1928. Fine and modest detail by the visionary explorer who persevered to "fly, fly, fly again."

Sir Hubert Wilkins, Lowell Thomas. New York: McGraw-Hill, 1961. The complete biography of Wilkins written in autobiographical style.

Brother to the Eagle, Erling Rolfsrud. Alexandria, MN: Lantern Books, 1952. Ben Eielson also died too young. This is the best biography of him.

My Polar Flights, Umberto Nobile. London: F. Muller, 1961. A gracious and ultimately convincing defense by the designer and master of the *Norge* and *Italia*.

The Italia *Disaster*, Rolf S. Tandberg. Oslo, Norway: Sorkedalsveien, 1977. In this brief but vital book, the inaccuracies, gossip, and slanders are neatly combed out.

Other Book Sources

Wings of Mystery, Dale M. Titler. New York: Dodd, Mead, 1966, rev. ed. 1981.

Two Against the Ice, Theodore Mason. New York: Dodd, Mead, 1982.

Struggle, Charles J. V. Murphy. New York: Fred A. Stokes, 1928.

Ships in the Sky, John Toland. New York: Holt, 1957.

Revolution in the Sky, Richard Allen Sanders. New York: Orion, 1988.

The Krassin, Maurice Parajanine. New York: Macaulay, 1929.

Periodical Sources

"The Fate of Andrée," *Geographical Journal*, November 1930.

"The Andrée Tragedy," Naboth Hedin. *American-Scandinavian Review*, November 1930.

"A Swedish Film Recreates a Daring Flight That Failed," R. T. Kahn. *Smithsonian*, May 1983.

"Andrée's Flight Into the Unknown," Jonas S. Stadling. *Century Magazine*, November 1897.

"Letters From the Andrée Party," Nils Strindberg and Family. *Century Magazine*, March 1898.

"Over the Top of the World," Vilhjalmur Stefansson. *American Magazine*, September 1928.

INDEX

R

Riesenberg, Felix, 19

Riiser-Larsen, Lt. Hjalmar, 42, 56, 99, 106

    on attempted airplane flight over North
        Pole, 31-34, 38-41

    on dirigible expedition, 58, 60, 61, 63,
        65, 66

Rockefeller, John D. Jr., 45, 48

Rolls-Royce engines, 32-34

Romagna Manoja, Giuseppe, 92, 95, 97, 100,
        101, 103

Rome, 57-58, 97, 98, 100, 101

Roosevelt, Theodore, 16

Russia, 21, 24

    see also Soviet Union

S

Samoilovitch, Rudolph, 103

SAS (Scandinavian Airlines System), 105

Schyberg, Birger, 100, 102

Scotland, 24

Scott, Robert F., 27, 52

Severnaya Zemlya, 92, 93

Shenandoah (dirigible), 41, 45

Skate (submarine), 107

Siberia, 8, 24, 28, 63, 105

South Pole, 1, 24, 27, 28, 34, 51, 55, 61, 65,
        106

Soviet Union, 70, 98, 106

Spitsbergen, 7-9, 13, 17, 20, 28, 32, 38, 41,
        45, 51, 74

    Amundsen-Ellsworth expeditions from,
        33, 34, 42, 43, 58-60

    Andrée at, 3-5

    Byrd's flight to North Pole from, 47-49,
        52-53

    discovery of, 2

    and Nobile's ill-fated expedition, 91, 92,
        94-97, 99

    Wellman at, 21, 22

    Wilkins-Eielson flight from Alaska to, 81-
        88

Stalin, Josef, 106

Stefansson, Vilhjalmur, 69, 71, 74, 80

Stinson Aircraft Company, 76-81

Strindberg, Nils, 5, 6-7, 9, *10*, 11, 13

Svalbard, *see* Spitsbergen

Svea (balloon), 4-5

Sweden, 5, 98

Swedish Air Force, 99

T

Teller, Alaska, 64, 66, 67

Tornberg, Egmont, 100

Trojani, Felice, 96, 100, 103

U

Uemura, Naomi, 105

Ultima Thule, 1

United States, 55, 57, 61

    dirigibles in, 45, 56, 98

    Peary claims North Pole for, 44

    Russian transpolar flights to, 105

    Wellman in, 21

U.S. Army, 2, 44

    Air Service, 71, 72, 89

U.S. Congress, 45

U.S. Naval Academy, 44

U.S. Navy, 41-43, 45-47, 106, 107

ABOUT THE AUTHOR

K. C. TESSENDORF WRITES:

"When I was a boy growing up in Wisconsin fifty years ago, I seldom failed to dash out of the house in unfailing wonder whenever I heard the drone of an airplane motor. And I can claim to have been nearer to a hurtling Ford trimotor aircraft than any person: My father incautiously parked in its landing path in a cow-pasture airfield. I was standing on our Chevy's running board and could have scratched a match on the plane's undercarriage as it flashed overhead! Surely that, plus WWII and Korean War tours of duty with the Air Force, had some part in sparking my interest in aviation."

K. C. Tessendorf has taken off with this interest in two of his previous books. *Wings Around the World* explores what it was like for U. S. Army fliers to fly around the world in the drafty, open-cockpit biplanes of the 1920s. *Barnstormers and Daredevils* tells the story of the freewheeling pilots of the same era who gave stunt rides in these biplanes to folks who had never seen an airplane before.

Mr. Tessendorf and his wife, Marlis, live in Falls Church, Virginia.